TEQUILA SUNRISE

AN AGENTS IRISH AND WHISKEY NOVELLA

LAYLA REYNE

D0556071

Tequila Sunrise

Copyright © 2017, 2023 by Layla Reyne

All rights reserved. No part of this book may be reproduced or transmitted in any form or by any means, electronic or mechanical, including photocopying, recording, or by any information storage and retrieval system without the written permission of the copyright owner, and where permitted by law. Reviewers may quote brief passages in a review.

Cover Design: Cate Ashwood Designs

Cover Photography: Lindee Robinson

1Ed Editing: Edits by Kristi, Deborah Nemeth

2Ed Editing: Adam Mongaya, Sandy Bennett

Second Edition

August 2023

E-Book ISBN: 978-1-962010-06-1

Paperback ISBN: 978-1-962010-07-8

This is a work of fiction. Names, characters, places, and incidents are either the product of the author's imagination or are used fictitiously. Any resemblance to actual persons living or dead, business establishments, events, or locales is entirely coincidental. All person(s) depicted on the cover are model(s) used for illustrative purposes only. The author acknowledges the copyrights and trademarked status and trademark owners of any trademarks and copyrights mentioned in this work of fiction.

Content Warnings: Explicit sex; explicit language; violence; instances and/or discussion of homophobia and racism.

ABOUT THIS BOOK

Melissa Cruz is the most dangerous woman alive. Post-FBI, the former Special Agent in Charge chases bounties and serves as chief of security for Talley Enterprises. She's also spent the past year falling in love with her best friend's little brother.

Daniel Talley never imagined the woman of his dreams would give him the time of day. Smart, fierce, and thirteen years his senior, Mel is way out of his league. But somewhere along the way of playing plucky sidekick, Danny finally caught Mel's attention.

What began as a little harmless flirting grew into so much more—and into a secret Mel and Danny have kept from their friends and family. But when the Talley flagship is hijacked, there's no keeping a lid on it any longer. Mel and Danny must rely on the trust they've built to rescue their loved ones and each other, or else it'll be a very unhappy Christmas Eve for all.

Tequila Sunrise is a standalone romantic suspense novella in the Agents Irish & Whiskey series. It features a fierce older woman, the reformed playboy who worships her, holiday hijinks and hijacks, and a heaping side of Irish & Whiskey cameos. This second edition features a new cover and formatting and extended content.

For Cory,
Because Die Hard is a fucking Christmas movie!

ONE

Fifteen minutes, not five.

That was how long it took any Jetway to reach its intended plane at SFO. While other first-class passengers rose around her, hauling luggage out of overhead bins and calling for rides, Mel remained seated. She stretched a long leg out in front of her, toeing over her rock-studded heels and slipping them on. Like her fellow travelers, she was in a hurry too—already a day late and less than two hours to showtime—but she knew the drill here at her home airport.

So too did the flight attendants on this daily hop from London. Her favorite steward, Jeremy, shuffled down the aisle at a leisurely pace, smiling. "Anything else, Agent Cruz?" he asked in his lilting accent. As was their routine, he handed over her folded suit jacket, the load noticeably lighter without her gun case tucked underneath.

"Just Ms. Cruz now," she said with as warm a smile as she could muster after flying all day.

"Old habits."

"Tell me about it." She was barely used to it herself, and she'd been out of the Bureau eight months now. If she had to change her name or title a third time, she'd shoot someone for sure.

Standing, she shrugged into her coat while Jeremy pulled her go bag and briefcase down from the bin. "See you next month?" he asked.

She bit back a truer grin as Jeremy adjusted his Santa hat. "Home for a bit," she managed.

On cue, her cell vibrated in her pocket. Expecting what was on it, she thought better than to pull it out in front of Jeremy. Thankfully, another passenger across the aisle signaled for his help.

"Duty calls," he said, extending a hand.

"Always a pleasure," she said, shaking it. "Have a happy holiday, Jeremy."

"Same to you, Ag—Ms. Cruz," he corrected before moving on.

Mel laid her bags in the empty window seat beside her and methodically went through the rest of her deplaning checks—swipe a hand through the seat back pocket, double-check around her seat, pat herself down to make sure she had everything, ignore the momentary flash of panic at the missing badge and gun. Personal effects all accounted for, she turned her back to the aisle and withdrew her phone.

You get here early enough you can have part one of your Xmas present before the party.

Below the text was a picture of her dark-haired, dark-eyed lover, looking like the sinful devil he was in a state of semiundress. Tuxedo pants hung low on his slim hips, an unbuttoned dress shirt showed off his long, lean torso, and a red and green bow tie dangled loose around his neck.

Oh so tempting. Danny knew what she liked to do with dangling pieces of fabric. At least it was around his neck in this shot. The picture he had sent eleven hours ago, as she'd sat in the boarding area at Heathrow, involved much less clothing, what looked like that same damn bow tie looped around his wrists, and the message, **Wouldn't you rather be on my plane?**

His fucking plane had been what started all this.

———

Sixteen Months Ago

It was the middle of the night when Mel charged into the private hangar, flashed her badge at the flight crew preparing the Talley jet, and marched up the portable stairs, banging down the airplane door until Danny answered.

As the boss and best friend of his brother, Aidan, Mel had been around Danny for a decade and a half. But the youngest Talley son was thirteen years her junior and always had a model on his arm or a phone to his ear, constantly on the go as Talley Enterprises' public face and COO. And he somehow managed to do all that with a permagrin that charmed everyone and irritated Mel to no end. That irritation had kept her from appreciating the rich boy player who had grown into a handsome, flirtatious, successful businessman.

But the Danny in front of her now, dressed only in a pair of low-slung sweats, she appreciated. Tall like the rest of the Talleys, his torso stretched for miles, and every one of those miles was delicious. Wide shoulders and a carved collarbone, a broad chest smattered with dark curls, lightly ribbed abs, and the most well-defined hip bones she had ever seen on a man. Not to mention the trail of dark curls leading below his waistband.

"See something you like?"

Gaze snapping up, she met that charming-bordering-on-shit-eating grin and grabbed hold of her remembered irritation. She shouldered him aside and barreled into the jet's main cabin. "I'm going with you. The first commercial flight out to Houston isn't until six, and I need to get to your brother sooner."

Danny scratched absently at his chest, leering when her goddamn betraying eyes strayed there. "Yeah, Mom called. Something about an incident this morning in Galveston. Good thing I was already going down there."

She tossed her bag onto the leather couch and put her hands on her hips. "And why was that?"

He crossed his arms, squaring off. And flexing. The devil. "Aidan asked me to gather some information. Shipping manifests and the like." He jutted his chin at a stack of folders on the table between two swiveling chairs. "He needed it in a hurry, and I had the connections to get it, without all those pesky law enforcement restrictions you're saddled with."

His pride, however well-deserved, was irritating too. A fucking hotshot civilian in the middle of a case that was bigger—and possibly more deadly—than any of them realized. "You couldn't just email those to him?"

"It seemed easier this way."

"To fly the company jet there in the middle of the night? That's not the real reason. Out with it, Daniel."

He startled a little, and an attractive blush slashed

across his high cheekbones. He didn't try to hide it, grinning wider. "I'm on a mission of my own. To check out this new partner of his."

"Oh, for fuck's sake." She dropped her arms and turned on her heel to keep from strangling him.

A second later, heat hit her back and his warm breath blanketed her ear. "Don't worry, chica. I'm not interested for myself. Just being a good brother, checking out this Jamie fellow."

She held up a commanding hand. "Don't say anything else."

"My lips are sealed, unless you want to do something about that."

She rolled her eyes but couldn't contain her laughter, surprised at the tiny bit of weight that floated off her chest with it. She glanced over her shoulder, nose to nose with the handsome devil. "You gonna give me a lift or what?"

"You gonna give me a date when we get back?"

"We'll see." She didn't think before she spoke—a rarity —and the spontaneity seemed to surprise Danny as much as it did her.

His dark eyes grew wide, his smile even wider. "I can work with that."

———

Present

Yes, she would rather have flown home on Danny's jet, but after spending the past week apart, being without him on the plane too, surrounded by all those memories, even for just the duration of the flight, would have been as frustrating as flying commercial.

And it would have given away the unscheduled stop she had made in Dublin for his Christmas present. She eyed her go bag in the seat, hoping like hell she hadn't overstepped.

The Jetway connected, bumping the plane and jolting her out of her thoughts. **Deplaning,** she messaged back. **Yacht or ship?**

The Ellen.

She did smile then, wide and true. The newest ship in the Talley Enterprises fleet, a major star at tonight's TE holiday party, had been named after the Talley matriarch. It had been a long-running family joke that there were ships named after each of the three Talley daughters and a few after the granddaughters too but none yet after Ellen. Danny's father, TE's CEO, swore he was saving the best for last, and that was certainly what would be on display tonight. A new flagship to vault TE ahead of its competitors and to send John into retirement with a happy life and a happy wife.

Everything set for tonight? she asked.

Everything's under control.

As TE's new chief of security, she was in charge of safety for tonight's event—from guest background checks to on-site security. Most of it was advance work, taken care of well before her trip, but she hadn't intended to cut her return so close. That said, her deputy security chief, Mitch, was a senior Talley employee, they had hired extra security for the event, and there would be no shortage of trained eyes at the party, with FBI agents Aidan and Cam and former agent Jamie all in attendance.

Need to run by my place and change, she texted. **Be there in 60.**

More like 90.

He was probably right. No longer having law enforcement clearance, she had to go through customs with the masses. But with only her briefcase, go bag, and gun case, which she now had to retrieve directly from TSA, she hoped to make it quick.

If we officially moved in together, this wouldn't be a problem, Danny added.

It was an argument they had been having for months. Between hectic work schedules and the news they hadn't told the family yet, she had kept her condo and he had kept his yacht, snatching time together at one place or the other but calling neither *their* home. They couldn't go on like this much longer, working or living the way they did. She realized that too and was as frustrated as Danny. But they weren't going to hash out a solution apart over texts. That was half their fucking problem.

Before she could reply, another text came through, blessedly letting her off the hook for now. **You don't need to swing by the condo. You've got your Sig. I've got everything else.**

Everything? she asked.

You put it all in a garment bag before you left. Dummy proof.

Danny proof.

Well, not the shoes . . .

Meaning he had gone for the highest pair of fuck-me heels in her closet—sparkly and stiletto, probably—versus the ones that actually matched her gown for the party.

Good.

After his bow tie teasing and a week away, she had the same idea. If she could make it to the port early.

She texted back **60** and pocketed the phone. Slinging her go bag over one shoulder, she picked up her briefcase and followed the rest of the first-class passengers off the plane, through international baggage claim, and into the customs cattle call. Six lines were separated by stanchions forming lanes that led to chest-high booths with customs agents sitting behind glass dividers. Guards stood behind each booth, ready for bag searches if the agent deemed it necessary. All the lanes funneled to the terminal exit behind the booths, with nowhere to go the other direction but back to the gates. She cased the entire area as she did every time through. No changes since last month.

Nearing the front of the line, motion ahead caught her attention. The agent manning her lane's booth left the box and another stepped in. None of the agents in the other lanes were relieved. Instincts tripped, an anticipatory shiver raced up Mel's spine, warning bells ringing in her ears, but with ropes on either side of her and a line of travelers behind her, she couldn't switch lanes or reverse direction without notice. She kept a watchful eye as she withdrew her passport and carry permit. When it was her turn, she stepped up to the booth and smiled politely, sliding her papers under the glass partition.

No longer traveling on a diplomatic visa, Mel's passport was new, as was her photo in it. Her hair in the picture and months later still was short and curly, the first time she'd worn it that way since Academy. It had been singed off by an explosion in April, and she'd kept it short, determined to live her life in a lower-maintenance way. And generally failing at it, hair notwithstanding.

The agent glanced up only long enough to make sure her person matched her passport. Typical inspector behavior. Maybe the original agent was just called into a meeting or away on an emergency. The agent scanned the passport under the electronic reader. "Nature of your visit?" he asked.

"Returning home."

"Of your travel?"

"Business."

The computer beeped once. Cleared. Two beeps and you were in trouble. Instead of handing back her documents, though, the agent looked up, his hazel eyes assessing. "What kind of business are you in, Ms. Cruz?"

"Shipping," she answered vaguely.

"And that required you to visit Croatia?"

"It did."

It did not, at least not in this instance. There was paperwork showing her in Dubrovnik on behalf of TE, but she had actually been in Vukovar on a contract assignment, chasing a war criminal no sanctioned government agency had been able to capture. She'd gotten her man, or rather, she had chased him into a snow-covered sunflower field where the very landmines he had planted during the war had claimed his miserable life.

Her fleeting sense of achievement was cut off as guards converged behind the booth agent. One held her gun case. The other wore a stern, determined expression. The warning bells in her head chimed louder.

"Is there a problem?" she asked.

The empty-handed guard came around the booth first. "If you'll come with us, Ms. Cruz." He held out an arm toward the adjacent holding rooms.

"May I ask what this is about?"

The one with her gun case came around the other side of the booth, boxing her in. "Routine checks."

She kept her voice neutral despite her growing alarm and impatience. "Gentlemen, I'm Melissa Cruz, the former Special Agent in Charge of the FBI's San Francisco field office, and now head of security for an international shipping company, which has its holiday gala this evening. I need to be going. As it's Christmas Eve, I'm sure there's someplace you'd rather be as well. My permits should be in the system and in order." She reached into the outer pocket of her briefcase and withdrew her get-out-of-jail-free card, handing it to the first guard. "If there are any issues, DOJ will clear them up for you."

He didn't bother to look at the card, just shoved it in his pocket. "Ma'am, please." The perfunctory *please* didn't rankle half as much as the condescending *ma'am*. Not that she wasn't used to the address, only that she was accustomed to hearing it with respect—or fear.

As two more guards approached, Mel assessed her options. She could take the four of them out right here, but that would only bring more guards. And more attention from the cattle pen full of witnesses who were already reaching for their phones, too used to airport disturbances these days. She had better odds from every angle if she moved this scene off the main floor.

She lifted her hands, palms out, de-escalating the situation. "Of course. Lead the way." She followed the guard with her gun case, while the other, after retrieving her documents from the booth agent, trailed behind them. Taking out her phone again, she texted Danny.

ICE not playing nice. Call Price. Gonna be late. Love you.

"We're going to need that too," the guard behind her said.

She expected as much, which was why she had pressed the side button after sending her text. When she tapped the darkened screen and brought up the unlock prompt, she entered the passcode Jamie had programmed into all their devices.

The screen darkened once more.

For good.

She handed it over her shoulder, hiding her smirk.

TWO

Danny finished knotting his bow tie and snagged his phone off the desk. Dark still. No more texts from Mel. He scrolled to her number and hit the call button. Straight to voicemail —not Mel's recorded voice—automated instead, reciting a random number generated by Jamie's embedded kill switch.

He turned the device end over end in his hand, giving himself reasons not to worry. Mel was on US soil, the most dangerous part of her job done. She had all the necessary paperwork and permits, never leaving for any gig without them. She could out-interrogate anyone, especially a couple of customs agents. She would serve them their balls for dinner, and if things got physical, he had no doubt her combat skills would win out. He had witnessed her take down multiple mercenaries at once, single-handed, without ever drawing a gun.

But the fact she had activated the kill switch, the fact she'd had him phone Nic Price at the US Attorney's Office, and the fact that sixty minutes had turned into ninety and now bordered on one-twenty, meant he was worried, regardless of all the reasons not to be.

This had to be karma, retribution for sleeping his way through his teens and twenties. *Don Juan Danny*, Mel had once called him. Then of course he had fallen for her, the resident badass who could break his neck as easily as she could break his heart. Which had almost happened in April when she'd nearly died, twice.

He could still remember her unconscious body, thrown against the wall and hair singed off by an explosion. And not twelve hours later, her blood, her life, pooling under his hand and staining her white sweater, bleeding out from the gunshot wound she had taken to save his brother and their niece.

Miraculously, she had pulled through, both times, and so had they, but Mel refused to be caged, and Danny knew they would never last if he tried to put her in one. Granted, he got a stomach ulcer for it, no matter how calm he seemed on the outside, but if that was the price he had to pay for being with her, so be it. Having come close to losing that love, to losing her, he didn't want to experience that awful feeling again for many, many years.

Years. They would have *years* together, a lifetime, he reassured himself as he tossed his phone on the desk.

His confidence waned, though, as the device landed next to the polished wood case he had brought out of the family safe. Reaching for it, he toggled the patina latch and carefully opened the lid. Nestled inside, cradled by green silk, were two gleaming silver pocket watches, inscribed with initials on one side and the Talley crest on the other, and in between them, an empty space for a third. Danny had thought he would have a lifetime with his older brother too. Not Aidan—Sean.

———

Thirty Years Ago

Danny squealed as his brother lifted him onto his shoulders, bringing him closer to the sky. He grabbed Sean's hair, holding tight, and stuck out his tongue, catching the cold, wet snowflakes falling from above. He laughed as his brother spun them round and round until the spinning made him feel sick. He patted Sean's head like he did Mama's cheek. "Down!"

He flew through the air again, off Sean's shoulders and into his lap as Sean sat in a patio chair. "You look green, baby bro," Sean said, tugging the scratchy scarf around Danny's neck tighter.

Danny tried to push it away, even though it was warm, until Sean held something shiny in front of his face. "Look at this, Danny," Sean said, and Danny forgot all about the scarf.

He liked shiny things. He reached out and ran his fingers over it. It was rough, not scratchy like the scarf, but not smooth like a spoon or like Mama's necklaces he liked to grab. He tried to grab hold of this new object, even though it was bigger than his hand.

"No, no, no." Sean laughed, holding it away from Danny. "It's too heavy for you just yet."

"What is it?"

"It's a watch." He mashed the top and it broke apart.

"Oh no! You broke it!"

"No, Danny, it's okay. Look, I just opened it. See? Open, close, open, close."

Sean was making the shiny part go away and come back, go away and come back. When it went away, there was another different shiny part with something dark, like a stick, moving on it.

"What's it do?"

"It tells time. You know, like the big clock in the corner of Da's office."

Danny made the noise the big clock made. "Ding, dong."

"That's right, but this one's smaller. I can carry it with me so I know when it's time to come home." He ruffled Danny's hair and pulled him closer. "Back to you."

Danny needed a watch too, then, to tell him time so he would know when to come home to his brother. "How's it work?"

Sean took Danny's hand in his and put it on the watch. He couldn't touch the moving parts, glass between his hand and them. "The arm"—Sean put their fingers on the stick piece—"goes around once each hour." He moved their fingers, round and round, like how they had spun. "And there are twenty-four times around in a day."

Danny yanked his hand back and stared up at Sean. "I want it."

"I'm sure you do." Sean snapped the first shiny part back on, and Danny reached for the watch again. Sean put it in his hand, but he couldn't hold it. "See," Sean said, catching it. "It's too big for you right now, but one day, you'll get one too."

"Me?" Danny said, looking up at his brother again.

Sean's eyes, the same color as his hair, the same as

Danny's and Da's, were shiny too. He kissed Danny's forehead. It was cold and wet like the snowflakes from the sky. "Yeah, baby bro, there's one waiting for you too."

Danny's eyes went back to the watch. "Open it," he said, repeating his brother.

Sean mashed the top again, and the shiny part went away again.

"Close it," he said, and Sean made it come back.

Over and over, open and close, until Danny laughed and clapped himself to sleep.

———

Present

That was the only memory Danny had of his oldest brother, his first memory ever, from a cloudy winter day right before his third birthday, right before Sean was killed by the IRA in a car bomb. The Garda Síochána, Ireland's police force, had seized Sean's personal effects at the crime scene, including his book bag and pocket watch, and Danny's family had fled Ireland before they could collect them. When Danny and Aidan had returned decades later, the Garda had said Sean's things were lost, like their brother, and the surviving brothers had kept their pocket watches in the family safe ever since. Danny had only pulled them out tonight in honor of his family's special occasion, though now Danny worried his doing so had been a curse.

His worry grew when Jamie entered the cabin, distress etched on his face.

Danny closed the lid on the box and pushed it aside. He wouldn't take his out until Aidan arrived, and judging by

Jamie's face, he guessed there was bad news on that front too. "Aidan?"

"Activated his kill switch."

Danny's stomach sank. Both Mel and his brother—Jamie's fiancé and acting SAC of the San Francisco field office—had gone dark.

"Any further word from Mel or Nic?" Jamie asked. He had gotten an auto notice when Mel activated her kill switch. Danny had told him it was a customs issue and that Nic was on top of it. But now with Aidan's activated too . . .

Danny shook his head. "Nothing. When did Aidan go offline?"

"A half hour ago at LAX. Didn't make his flight."

"Where's Cam?" Danny asked, referring to Aidan's new partner.

"On deck running through security protocols with your security deputy." Head down, Jamie was already typing a text.

Danny could read Nic's name on the screen. "You think it's related to the party tonight?" he asked.

"I hope not, but the timing is suspicious."

Danny's stomach bottomed the rest of the way out. He closed his eyes and lifted his hands to run them through his hair, then, at the last possible second, remembered it was styled and balled his hands into fists instead. His parents, siblings, and friends of the family were here. TE's investors and employees were here. Members of the financial and tech press were here. If something happened tonight, everything—everyone—was in jeopardy.

"Hey." Jamie lightly grasped his arm. "The wheels are in motion. Nic's at SFO"—he flashed the phone at him, displaying Nic's curse-laden confirmation—"the LA SAC is headed to Aidan, and Cam is coordinating here. You and I both know if Mel and Aidan want out of whatever boxes they're being held in, they'll find a way out. Our bases are covered."

"What do we do? Just go out there and pretend nothing's wrong?"

"Nothing may be wrong," Jamie replied. "If it is, panicking a ship full of fancy-dressed people won't do us a damn bit of good. I'll go out there and keep my eyes open with Cam." He swiped back his tux jacket to reveal a gun at his waist, which eased another fraction of Danny's tension. "You go out there and be Daniel Talley, charming, funny COO of Talley Enterprises. Future CEO, once your dad retires. This is as much your commissioning as it is this ship's."

Danny tipped his head. "Nice use of nautical terms."

"I've learned a few spending the last six months designing software for this baby." He patted the wall, smiling. "And I did spend many a summer with Cam's family on the water." Jamie stepped closer, pulling a long narrow item from inside his coat pocket. "Aidan and I were going to give this to you at the end of the night, but I think it'll give you some comfort now."

The slim black case Jamie handed him was top-of-the-line leather, hand-stitched and embossed with his initials and the TE clover and star logo. Danny folded back the flap and ran his fingers over the polished tension wrench, pick, and rake inside.

Lock pick tools.

Comfort indeed.

"And now you can get yourself out of any box too," Jamie said.

Danny drew him into a crushing hug. "Thank you, Jameson, for everything."

"You're welcome." Jamie gave him two backslaps before stepping back. "Now, your guests are arriving and we're due onstage soon. Let's mingle."

Mingle. Right. And trust that the bases were covered. He had the best in the security business on his staff and in his family. They should be good, safe. He slid the new lock pick set inside his jacket pocket, ran a hand over the box of watches, and grabbed his phone off the desk. Still dark. He dropped it in his pants pocket where it made a muffled clank against Mel's gift.

He put on the smile that had stolen a thousand hearts, praying that the one and only holder of his would be here soon.

THREE

Mel had tried polite. She had tried persuasive. She was two seconds from trying—and no doubt succeeding at—combative when Nic charged through the door.

"Someone want to tell me what's going on here?" the prosecutor demanded.

The single guard sitting across the table from her stood, finally speaking for the first time since he had closed the door behind them. "Who are you?"

Nic tossed his ID wallet at him. "Assistant US Attorney Dominic Price." In all his steely-eyed, well-dressed, legal eagle glory. There was a reason Mel had always requested Nic on her cases. He was the best closer in San Francisco's US Attorney's Office. Better than the US Attorney himself. And he was a trusted friend. "What are the charges against Ms. Cruz?"

"He's the one whose card I gave you," Mel added. "You didn't call him, which means he's extra angry now." Arms folded, she leaned back in her chair, crossing one knee over the other, foot bouncing.

The guard handed back Nic's ID. "DOJ doesn't call the shots here."

"Correct, but what DOJ does do, including my office, is defend cases by travelers against ICE and Homeland Security for unlawfully holding them." Nic glanced over his shoulder. "Ms. Cruz, will you be bringing a case?"

"I'm definitely considering it."

He turned back to the guard. "So, I ask you again, on what grounds are you holding Ms. Cruz?"

"There are irregularities with her passport and travel." The guard shifted on his feet and clasped his hands behind his back. Hiding his fidgeting fingers, Mel suspected, and something else she sensed she would need to get to the bottom of.

"What kind of irregularities?" Nic said.

"Frequent travel, including to suspect countries."

"Ms. Cruz, what is it you do for a living?"

"She's already told us that," the guard said.

"Then you know why she travels extensively."

"She travels with a gun."

"Which she is permitted to carry, because as you also know, she's a former FBI agent."

"Next question," Mel said, shifting forward and bracing her forearms on the table. "Who do you work for?"

The guard's gaze whipped to her. "ICE, Department of Homeland Security."

She narrowed her eyes. "Who do you really work for?"

"Answer the lady," Nic said. "Maybe it'll help me defend you because from where I'm standing, you've got no grounds for holding her."

The guard shifted on his feet again, appearing on the edge of debate—let her go, dig in his heels, or call his boss, legitimate or otherwise, for direction. Another split glance between her and Nic, and the guard chose option three, as Mel expected him to. "I'll just be a minute," he said and slipped out the door.

Before Mel said a word, Nic gave his head a barely there shake. Meaning that mirror on the opposite wall was likely a two-way and they were being observed. "Thank you for coming, Price," she said, guarding her words.

He propped himself against the adjacent wall. "You're welcome."

The guard returned shortly with her documents, bags, and gun case, setting all her belongings on the table. "You're free to go, Ms. Cruz."

As she should have been two hours ago, but arguing now was besides the point. She needed to get out of this room and get to the *Ellen*. She gathered her things and exited through the door Nic held open. As soon as they were in his truck and clear of the parking garage, she shifted in her seat, angling toward him. "Report."

"Nothing amiss at the party yet. Boston's running point with your deputy." He tossed his phone into her lap. "Text them. Tell them we're on our way."

She sent her message in the open group chat—**It's Mel. Out of SFO. On our way**—then read the flurry of other messages above hers.

"Aidan's been detained at LAX?"

Nic nodded. "He didn't make it onto his flight."

The phone vibrated in her hand, an incoming text from a burner phone.

In-flight LAX to OAK. Tell Mom and Dad I'm sorry for being late.

Aidan.

Gracias a Dios. "He's in flight now," she said. "Direct into Oakland."

Nic drummed his thumbs on the steering wheel as they sped north on 101. "Good, that's both of you clear, then."

Mel could see how her travel record might raise some flags, especially if anyone looked deeper or got wind of her off-book activities. But Aidan too . . . "This can't be coincidence."

"If it is, it's an awfully big one."

Not likely. Coincidences like this didn't just happen. Not to them. At least in this case, she had a place to start. "I'm going to need another favor," she said.

"The guard," Nic correctly surmised.

"We find out who he works for, we find out what the hell is going on."

FOUR

Jazzy Christmas tunes played as Danny worked the crowd on the *Ellen*'s deck. Next week, this area would be piled high with shipping containers for the cargo vessel's maiden voyage, but tonight it was more shiny and sparkly than he would ever see it again. Trimmed in garland, bows, and twinkling white lights, with standing heaters spaced every ten feet or so, the deck glowed and overflowed with holiday cheer. Not to mention all the finery in human form. Waiters carried trays of caviar canapés and champagne among guests dressed in tuxedos and gowns, couples twirled on the two parquet dance floors set up over the reinforced hatches, and on the bow, at the opposite end of the deck, his mother and father stood on a raised dais, toasting glasses among family and friends.

They'd had onboard TE parties over the years—for commissionings, retirements, and holidays—but never anything this extravagant. Then again, they had never had a commissioning, retirement, or holiday quite like this one.

The commissioning of a vessel designed to hold more

while traveling faster and cleaner than any other ship in its class, with custom-designed tech that allowed customers to pinpoint the exact location of their goods in transit and to preclear them through customs.

The retirement of Danny's father, the company's founder, who had left an empire behind and fled Ireland after Sean was killed, rebuilding a bigger and better shipping empire here in the States.

A holiday party capping off one of TE's best years and one of the Talleys' best too. Near-deaths notwithstanding, the ever-growing army of redheaded grandchildren was happy and healthy, Aidan had found love again and proposed to Jamie, and Danny had settled down with Mel.

They had so many reasons to celebrate, and Danny played the part well, clinking champagne glasses, shaking hands, and making smiling small talk, even as his insides churned. He was not the same carefree, thrill-seeking Danny of a year ago. The one who had butted in on Bureau matters, who had blithely tagged along to defuse a bomb with Mel and Aidan, who had wooed a paralegal so Jamie could get access to files. That Danny's bravado had waned while sitting vigil at Mel's hospital bedside, listening for the slightest change in her heartbeat that would spell his doom. Now, the silence of his phone, despite the cacophony of noise around him, was equally terrifying.

Finishing the conversation he had already checked out of, Danny moved toward the stage, gaze bouncing left and right, searching for any sign of Mel and Aidan and, when he didn't find them, for Jamie and Cam. Jamie, inches taller than everyone else, was a few feet away, his posture on alert. After another few seconds searching, he located Cam, the agent sticking out as one of the few men in a suit rather than a tux. He stood halfway up the deck, stationed near the green-carpet gangway that led to the pier. Cam's dark eyes shifted from the arrived guests on deck, to the arriving guests on the gangway, to the pier and parking lot beyond, watching for the two people they most wanted to see.

Until suddenly Cam's attention snapped back around and down to the phone in his hand. Jamie likewise jolted into motion. And when his own phone vibrated, Danny startled too. Digging it out of his pocket, he saw the screen lit with a text from Mel at Nic's number. A smile spread across Danny's face, a real one, as he breathed easy for the first time in hours. It grew wider when another message came through on the heels of Mel's, this one from Aidan on a burner number. He was on his way too.

Danny glanced up as Jamie's entire being sagged with relief. He made his way over and laid a hand on the big man's shoulder. "I think I can finally drink this and enjoy it." Danny tilted his champagne glass toward Jamie's. "Cheers."

Jamie chuckled, tapping his full glass against Danny's. "Cheers, indeed."

Cam joined their group as Danny swapped his glass out for a fresh one. He swiped a second and handed it to the agent. "If the threat has passed, drink up."

"I'm not convinced it has." Cam sipped, badly hiding a grimace.

"Or you just don't like champagne."

"Or fancy parties," Jamie added.

"Please tell me I don't have to wear a monkey suit at the wedding."

Jamie grinned. "It's called a morning jacket, and it has tails."

"Jesus fucking Christ." The curse came out extra thick in Cam's Boston brogue before he washed it down with the entire glass of champagne, face contorting.

Danny laughed, slapping Cam's back. "Nic's brewery is providing kegs for the big day. I'll make sure your pint glass stays full."

"See," Cam said, eyes narrowed at Jamie, "Danny-boy's a real friend."

"You do know that was a fifty-dollar glass of champagne, right?"

Cam nearly choked and Danny laughed louder.

He wished Mel was here to share the moment. After what had to have been a long day, the laugh would do her good, as would the champagne—her favorite, Bollinger. He had learned that nugget of information by accident on their way back from Galveston.

Sixteen Months Ago

As they prepared the jet for departure, Danny slipped a couple hundred-dollar bills into one of the ground crew's hands. "See if you can get our neighbor over there"—he nodded toward the other G5 in the hangar—"to part with a bottle of whatever bubbly they've got onboard."

"You got it, boss," the crewman said. He scurried off, flagging down another guy in a utility jacket and giving him a complicated handshake by which Danny guessed money was exchanged. The neighboring crewman disappeared onto the plane, then reappeared after a minute with a noticeable bulge under his vest. A poorly disguised handoff later and Danny's man brought back a bottle of

Bollinger, along with one of the hundreds. "Saved you some cash too."

Danny took the bottle and left the bill. "You keep that. For your trouble." The crewman smiled, shook his hand, and Danny headed up the stairs. Inside, he stashed the bottle in the onboard chiller before taking his seat, ignoring Mel's eyes tracking him across the cabin while she rattled off orders to someone on the phone.

Later, the pilot announced they had reached cruising altitude just as she hung up.

"Was that a bottle of champagne you tried to sneak in here?" she asked.

He unbuckled his seat belt and walked over to retrieve it. "I wasn't trying to sneak anything." He grabbed the bottle, a towel, and two crystal flutes from the built-in minibar and brought them to where Mel sat on the bench seat. "How about that date now?"

"I don't believe I ever agreed to one," she countered, even as she took the glasses from him.

He popped the cork on the bottle. "Yes, well, no matter how good you are at getting out of binds, and let me just say, as frightening and impressive as that display of combat skills was today, I do believe this"—he gestured at the cabin around them, where they would be confined for the next few hours—"is the definition of captive audience."

"Maybe I should be commending you on *your* display of skills today. When did you start picking locks?"

He finished filling the glasses, wrapped the base of the bottle with the towel, and placed it in the cubby in the ledge behind the couch. "Eight," he said, lowering himself next to her. "By ten, I was better than my teacher."

"Let me guess. Aidan?"

He tilted his glass for a toast, and she clinked the crystal rims together before taking a sip. Her muted moan of pleasure was an unexpected torture, in his pants and elsewhere. "What did you need to pick locks for at that age?" she asked.

He didn't hide his leer, remembering exactly to what use he had put those skills, stealing certain magazines out of the older boys' lockers at school.

"Dios mío. I don't want to know."

"All in good fun," he said before taking a swallow.

"If that's what you call it," she said, chuckling. "But seriously, Daniel, you did good today. You kept your cool."

It was all he could do not to preen under her praise. "Well, I couldn't look like the hapless civilian next to James Bond and M."

She twirled the stem of the flute with her delicate, deadly fingers. "I did always have a fondness for Bollinger."

He stretched out an arm over the seat back behind her, and she didn't flinch or move away, but rather leaned into it. He took that as a sign, a very good one. "Think you might be developing a fondness for me, M?"

"I don't know, Q, maybe." She smirked, affectionate and playful, and Danny thought maybe that was the second he fell.

The next second, when her lips met his, he was gone for good.

———

Present

His father's *tap, tap, tap* on the dais microphone jarred

Danny out of the memory. "Family, friends, can I have your attention, please."

Tall and strapping, dark eyes glittering and lively, his father looked far from seventy, only his thick mane of hair, gone from black to silver to white over the past few years, giving him away. Danny hoped he looked as good at that age. But it wasn't just the healthful appearance Danny aspired to. John stood tall, proud, and happy, with an arm around his glowing wife of fifty years. That sort of fulfillment, professional and personal, was what Danny wanted. And he knew who he wanted it with, Mel's gift in his pocket the next step in getting that life.

"I want to thank you all so much for joining us here tonight," his father began in his still-heavy Irish accent. "This is the biggest party I can ever remember throwing, and I've had six children and six grandchildren—"

"Seven," Danny's sister Grace, who had just that year had another child, shouted behind him onstage.

"Seven grandchildren," he corrected with a hearty laugh, "to throw parties for over the years. Not to mention all the weddings."

Danny jostled Jamie's arm, and Jamie hid his smile behind a gulp of champagne.

"Now I know you all want to get back to eating, drinking, and dancing, but Daniel—where are you, Daniel?" His father peered out over the crowd.

"Oh!" Danny raised his hand. "That's my cue."

"My son has some wonderful shipping advancements to tell you about in a little bit."

The crowd looked to him, politely clapping, then back to his father.

"But as this will likely be the last chance I have to

address all of you, I wanted to take this opportunity to thank a few people. First, to the TE employees here tonight and all throughout the years, you helped me rebuild this dream from the ground up, with your time and effort and heart, and here we are today, number one, because of you." He held his arms out wide to raucous applause. "Next, to my family, who are the greatest joys of my life, and who have and will keep this company, my other great joy, running."

He made sure to make eye contact with Danny and each of his siblings. All of them except Aidan were in the family business.

"And finally, to my wife, Ellen, who in the darkest days of our lives held our family together, moved us across the pond, and convinced me I could do this again." John held her tight to his side, grinning down with affection Danny felt in his heart a deck-length away. "I did it, mo chroí, because you said I could, and I saved the best for last. Merry Christmas. I hope you like your ship." He bent down as she stretched up on her toes, the two of them kissing, as much in love in their golden years as they had been as teens.

The partygoers cheered so loudly Danny didn't hear the errant noise at first. But the men on either side of him did, their relaxed bearing vanishing. Seeing them tense, Danny tuned out the crowd, straining to hear and see what they did, and a low *whoomp-whoomp-whoomp*, like propellers, registered first. Then, following Jamie's and Cam's gazes to the sky, he spotted the dark mass with a single red taillight off in the distance.

Approaching fast.

"I didn't see a flyover listed on the program," Jamie

said.

"Because there isn't one. Why would we do that at night?" Danny's stomach resumed its somersaults, sloshing champagne. "Maybe it's military. Not uncommon with all the bases around."

On the phone already, Cam rattled off his name, title, and badge number. "I need to know who's got clearance to fly a chopper over Port of Oakland tonight."

Guests around them started to notice the disturbance, glancing skyward, but an equal number paid it no mind. Like he'd told Jamie and Cam, late-night flyovers weren't unheard of, though come to think of it, those were usually closer to midnight. And the approaching chopper was flying directly at them, the *whoomp* of the propellers and *growl* of the engines growing louder by the second.

"There's a reason Mel and Aidan were held up, wasn't there?" Danny said, putting two and two together.

Cam lowered his phone. "No scheduled flights over the port tonight."

Helicopter almost on them, the *whoomp* and *growl* drowned out the music and drew everyone's attention. "I need to get to my family!" Danny shouted.

Cam put a hand to his chest and shoved him back into Jamie, whose muscled arm wrapped around his chest from behind. "I'll secure the family," Cam said to Jamie. "Get him clear!" Cam rushed off, plowing through the crowd to the far edge, while Jamie dragged Danny backward. People scattered around them, ducking low and covering their heads, as the helicopter hovered overhead.

Black, no lights, no markings.

All signs pointed to no good.

Onstage, his father directed traffic, rushing people off

the dais and handing their mother over to his sisters and their husbands. Danny needed to be with them. "I've gotta go!" he hollered, trying to wrestle free from Jamie. "Let me go!"

Jamie pointed toward the gangway. "Danny, look."

Confused, anxious party guests were being herded back on board by armed men dressed in black. Mercenaries, judging by the trail of TE security guards left in their wake as they stormed up the plank.

Danny gasped. "What the fuck is going on?"

"Someone's hijacking this party," Jamie replied.

Proving his point, ropes unfurled from the chopper, and the crowd shifted from confused and anxious to full-on panic, running for the blocked exits. Danny needed to do something. He was TE's COO, the CEO as of tomorrow. This was his party, his company, his family. And yet fucking Jamie kept hauling him backward. "Dammit, J, I need to go!"

"You need to stay out of sight so we keep our advantage." Jamie spun him around and clutched both his shoulders. "You're apart from the rest of the family. Designated survivor." Danny's stomach lurched and he nearly puked on Jamie's shoes. Jamie palmed his cheek, steadying his gaze. "And you're the most valuable as far as skills. I need your help, baby bro. Can you help me?"

Jamie's use of Sean's and Aidan's nickname for him steadied Danny. Made him focus on the other words Jamie had said.

Help.

Skills.

Jamie was right. He was more useful apart with Jamie, picking a lock and handling the crisis. Across the deck, Cam was securing his family, dispersing them into the crowd, pairing each with a tuxedoed Talley security guard, a redundancy safety measure Mel had insisted on. Cam was hiding them in plain sight, protected, among the other guests, as the mercs flooded the stage and surrounded the crowd.

Danny nodded. "We need to call Mel and Aidan."

"After I get you clear." Jamie pushed him toward the bridge stairs, hand on his shoulder, forcing him low as they scrambled up.

Two steps from the top, a familiar voice halted Danny in his tracks.

"Ladies and gentlemen, if you'll remain calm, no harm will come to you." The speaker was a woman, as evidenced by her voice and by her stunning face and long blond hair, unveiled as she ripped off her helmet and mask.

Many in the crowd gasped. They knew her too, though perhaps not as intimately as Danny did.

"Who is she?" Jamie asked, catching on to his and the crowd's recognition.

"Sonja Lynch," Danny answered. "Head of Lynch Shipping. TE's biggest competitor."

FIVE

Bile stung the back of Danny's throat, champagne and caviar threatening a reappearance, as Jamie shoved him through the swinging door to the bridge. Danny automatically reached for the light switch, and Jamie slapped his hand away.

"Lights off," Jamie whispered low. "And keep your head down."

Crouching, they snuck to the center of the bridge, neither of them needing light, familiar as they were with the *Ellen*. Danny reached up an arm, ran a hand over the control panel, and pressed the button to open the speakers, allowing them to hear the commotion below.

Jamie tapped his shoulder and held up a single digit, then two, silently asking one-way or two.

"Just receiving," Danny confirmed.

Through the speakers, Sonja shouted orders over panicked cries, directing her hired guns.

"Reel in the gangways."

"Close all the doors."

"Block any exit."

"No one in or out."

To Danny's further astonishment, the orders were relayed down the line by Mitch. He would know that deep, rumbly voice anywhere, having heard it since he was a kid.

Party guests shouted "Sonja!" or "Mitch!" together with some variety of "What the fuck is going on?"

Danny filtered out the anger, betrayal, and fear roaring in his ears and listened closely. None of the panicked voices belonged to his family. Were they silenced by the guards— being dragged onstage as he hid—or were they following Cam's orders and lying low in the crowd? He prayed for the latter.

Beside him, Jamie opened a door beneath the control panel and began connecting wires directly to his phone.

"What are you doing?" Danny asked.

"Hacking the system and locking down the computers," he answered, not looking up from his phone. "Better question, what the hell is Lynch doing? And why is Mitch helping her?"

"I have no idea. Mitch has been with TE for twenty years, and I've only ever seen Sonja in the boardroom." He hesitated on the cusp of full disclosure, but given the circumstances . . . "And the bedroom."

Jamie glanced up, brow raised. "How long ago?"

"Business school," Danny answered.

"How did it end?"

"With a bottle of Dom and a spectacular goodbye fuck. She was headed to open the family office in London. She was still in London, as far as I knew, running the operation from there."

"So you have no idea—"

Before Jamie finished, Sonja's voice rang out, calling the crowd to attention and giving them the last explanation Danny expected.

"We're here for the Talleys, or I should say, the IRA is."

Sonja Lynch was IRA? Since when? Danny's head spun as she railed on.

"They've lived and prospered here with the blood of our brothers on their hands. The Talleys owe us a price, and that price is blood."

Three decades had passed before the IRA wanted revenge?

No, this could not be happening. The IRA had killed Sean, and Danny's family had run, been granted asylum, and started a new life and empire in the US. The IRA couldn't come back for them. Not now. Not here. Not on his father's, his family's, big night.

"Danny! Danny!" Jamie waved a big hand in front of his face, snapping him out of his spiral. "Did you know she was IRA?"

He blinked, focusing. "Fuck no. She was born and raised here."

"Family, then, or some other connection?"

"Her last name is Irish, but I thought that was as far as it went." Sonja didn't have any trace of an accent, nor did any of her family members he had met.

"You said they had a London office?" Jamie said.

"Yes, but the company was founded in the US. It never existed in Ireland like TE. Sonja took them overseas when she opened London."

Jamie set his phone on the floor, lines of code streaming across the screen, and held out a hand. "Give me yours."

"Who are you calling?"

"Our only outside line at the moment." He hit speaker and the ringing dial tone filled the bridge, albeit quieted as Jamie lowered the volume.

Nic answered on the second ring. "Price."

"Put us on speaker," Jamie said. "I've got Danny with me."

"And I've got Mel," Nic said.

She added a "Jamie," then "Daniel," the second a touch softer, and Danny's heart took a break from hammering in fear, thumping with longing instead.

He had loved the way his given name rolled off her tongue for sixteen years, since the first time he had met Melissa Cruz.

————

Sixteen Years Ago

Danny faintly heard someone call his name, but it was far enough away not to concern him. Or the caterer's assistant who had his hand down Danny's pants, jerking him off, while Danny likewise returned the favor. He just hoped the Christmas music on the other side of the pantry door covered their grunts long enough for them to finish. Mr. Sexy in an Apron wasn't much older than him. It wouldn't take them long.

"Fuck, I'm gonna come," the hot blond groaned. "Fuck."

Danny added a twist to his stroke, teased the other guy's slit with his thumb, and panted in his ear, "Do it." That did the trick, just like with the other dudes he'd fooled around with. Sticky wet heat filled his palm and with a "Fuck yeah" of his own, Danny came too. His load seeped through his fingers around their cocks, dripping over his balls and onto his thigh. He slumped against the door, catching his breath and the other guy's body against his.

Hazy blue eyes stared up at him. "Fuck, that was good."

"Yeah," Danny agreed. "Just what I needed." He loved his family, he really did, but Aidan was late to the Christmas party, which meant he'd had no one to run interference for him. No one to deflect his parents' lofty expectations and no one to quash his sisters' doomed setups. He was a semester away from high school graduation, a summer between that and his freshman year of college. He wasn't looking for anything serious, future- or relationship-wise. He was looking for fun, like the sort he'd just had.

"Sorry if I made a mess," Blue Eyes said.

"Don't be," Danny said. "I can sneak up the back stairs and change."

A fist pounded on the door at his back. "Baby bro! You in there?"

Or not.

"Shit!" The assistant scrambled back, getting adorably tangled in his apron as he raced to pull it back around and zip his pants. He smeared his come-covered hand all over the smock, and Danny's last thought before the door was yanked open was that the dude better change that apron before going back to work.

He ducked his head and skirted past Danny, mumbling apologies. Unhurried, Danny zipped his dress pants, wiped his sticky hand on his hip, and turned. If there was anyone who wouldn't judge him, it was Aidan.

Except Aidan wasn't alone.

Beside his brother stood the most beautiful woman Danny had ever seen. She had legs for days, curves in all the right places, springy dark curls that were teased to perfection, and dark brown eyes that were inviting and terrifying all at once. Dressed in a sultry red number that showed off enough of her brown skin to be both sexy and modest, she had painted her lips to match, and they were quirked in a smirk that mirrored his brother's.

"Danny," Aidan said. "This is Melissa Cruz, the Academy classmate I told you about. Mel, this my brother, Daniel Talley, in all his horny teenage glory."

Those dark brown eyes glittered with amusement. "Daniel."

If he hadn't just come, Danny would have then at the way she said his name. Would have made a mess—

Fuck, a mess.

He glanced down at the dark stain on his hip, the bigger one over his crotch, and the trailing stain down his left pant leg.

His face caught fire, and he was sure it was as red as Mel's dress. He briefly contemplated doing the same as his hookup—keeping his head ducked, skirting past them, then sprinting up the stairs to his room where he could die of embarrassment. But that wasn't who he was. Never had been, never would be.

So he raised his chin, met the gorgeous woman's stare, and extended the hand not still sticky with leftover come. "Danny," he said, shaking her hand and trying not to wither under the strength of her grip. "Seventeen and horny, at your service."

She laughed out loud, and Danny thought right then that if he was ever going to get serious about someone someday, it would be this woman.

Present

"We've got a situation here," Jamie said, bringing Danny back to the present. "How far out are you?"

"Bay Bridge," Mel answered. "A chopper just flew overhead. That wasn't on the program tonight."

Danny found his voice again. "Neither was the IRA."

"What?" Mel and Nic said together.

Jamie filled them in on the last few chaotic minutes while Danny racked his brain for any Lynch-IRA connections, trying and failing to wrap his head around the situation. Sure, Sonja was a shark, but she had never been a militant one nor an ideological one. Profit was the bottom line. Had she been recruited in London? Was there some deeper connection he didn't know about?

Worse than answering the swirling questions, though, was battling his every instinct that screamed for him to make a break for the door, to get out there and rescue his family.

"Where are the rest of the Talleys?" Mel said, as if hearing his inner torment.

Jamie clasped his arm, also anticipating his escape. "On deck with Cam."

Two sharp inhales on the other end of the line. "What about Mitch?" Mel asked, recovering first. "The security teams?"

"The team members who weren't taken out by Lynch's mercs are paired up with Talleys in the crowd," Jamie said. "Cam's hiding and guarding them."

"And Mitch is standing next to Sonja onstage," Danny

said, answering the rest of her question, not hiding the betrayal and disgust that laced his voice.

Jamie waited for Mel's string of Spanish curses to end, then asked, "What's the plan?"

Even though she wasn't a fed anymore, Mel went into full SAC mode, dishing out orders. "Jamie, you're my eyes and ears. Nic, add Lynch and Mitch to the list for deep background checks. Daniel, you stay with Jamie."

Danny wrenched his arm free. "That's my family, my company, out there."

"It's mine too," Mel replied, and some of the fight went out of him. As much as it killed him to sit here in the bridge, at least he had eyes and ears on the situation. He could only imagine Mel's frustration and impatience at not being on the scene. She had risked life and job for his family, worked for this company, and considered both her own. As they were.

And God help them all once Aidan learned what was going on.

"I won't lose you," Mel said, and Danny hung his head, adrenaline rushing out, the weight of it all slamming into his gut. "Danny," Mel called, and he glanced back at the screen, as if he could see her there. "I need you to be smart and stay out of sight."

He shook his head, not that she could see him either. "Don't fucking sideline me, chica."

"I know better than that. I need you out of sight, for now, so you're still in play later when *I* need you."

"Need me for what?"

"To do what you do best. Unlock some doors for me."

Danny's heart leapt, pounding his ribs, an equal mix of anticipation and fear. He laid a hand over it and over the brand-new lock pick set in his coat pocket. Mel wasn't sidelining him. She needed him.

"We're going to save them," she said.

Anticipation and hope eclipsed fear, and Danny couldn't help but smile.

Sonja Lynch had no idea what she was in for.

SIX

A pier over from where the *Ellen* was docked, Nic swung his truck into a parking spot and killed the engine. "You're not going to wait for backup, are you?"

Mel reached behind his seat for her gun case. "Would you if it was your loved ones at risk?" As she righted herself, she didn't miss the clench of his jaw, teeth grinding loud enough to hear in the otherwise silent cab.

He opened the console between their seats and withdrew a Ka-Bar and Beretta. "Then I'm going in as your backup."

The ex-Seal would be the best backup she could ask for, probably better than any she'd had in the Bureau. But she needed Nic's cool, calm demeanor on the outside for an even more difficult task. She flipped open the gun case and pulled out her SIG Sauer P220, then, from under the foam, a box of ammunition and three magazines. "I've got Jamie on the inside," she said. "I need you out here."

Sirens echoed in the distance, their number and volume increasing. With that many people on board, multiple guests had no doubt called 911 as soon as the chaos had erupted.

"You need me coordinating with local authorities," Nic surmised.

Yes, but that would be a cakewalk compared to the other favor she needed. She took the knife and gun from him and added it to her arsenal. And depriving him of their use against her. "I also need you to keep Aidan from coming on board."

Nic slammed a hand against the steering wheel. "Dammit, Cruz! You just said there was no holding you back when your loved ones were at risk." He jutted a finger toward the windshield, toward the twinkling lights of the *Ellen* glowing on the water. "That's Aidan's family in there. Jamie's in there."

"And Aidan's the last adult Talley left out here."

"I thought Danny was the designated survivor."

"Danny's on that ship." Danny, who she hadn't seen in over a week, who she hadn't seen more than half the days of their relationship. All she had wanted to do tonight was come home and kiss him, tell their family the good news, then figure out a way to see more of each other. Now, though, she faced the very real possibility of never seeing him again. Unless she resurrected her SAC face and got everyone in line. She pushed through the lump in her throat. "With the IRA involved, we can't assume anyone on the *Ellen* is a survivor."

Fear flashed in Nic's icy blues. He covered the reveal quickly, redirecting his gaze out to the water. Mel wondered if she was asking more of Nic than to merely handle background searches, the authorities, or Aidan. She was asking him to stand down when she wouldn't.

"I've got this, Dominic," she said, squeezing his arm. "That's my family in there. I'm not going to let anything happen to them or anyone else on that ship."

"Fine," he said after a long pause, steely gaze swinging back to her. "I'll *try* to keep Aidan on shore."

That was the best any of them could hope for concerning Aidan. She reached into the inner pocket of the gun case and withdrew four comm devices, testing each as she spoke. "Aidan's also the Bureau's acting SAC here. You and he are two of the DOJ's top-ranking officials in the area. I need you both to keep the local cops from doing anything that jeopardizes more lives."

"Good, that'll give Aidan a target besides me." Nic shoved his door open, gravel crunching beneath his feet as he stalked toward the back of the truck.

Mel tossed her case behind the seats, collected her arsenal, and followed. Standing, she stashed the extra mags in her pockets and hooked the knife sheath's leather loop around her belt, the heavy counterweight comforting.

Nic stood at the side of the truck, rifling through the mounted toolbox. A few clanks and bangs later, he surfaced with a burner phone, another pistol, and two loaded mags. "Commando up," he said, holding them out to her.

After double-checking the safety, she tucked the extra gun in her back waistband along with the Beretta, cinched the extras mags tight with her belt, and paired one of the comm devices with the phone. She nestled the comm in her right ear, pocketed another and the phone, then handed two earpieces to Nic. "One for you, the other for Aidan. Radio as soon as you find anything or if the cops decide to storm the gates."

"I'm not worried about the cops."

And they were back to Aidan. She had one more lever to pull there. "The grandkids are at home tonight. Tell Aidan to stay onshore for them." All the Talley grandchildren were at risk of losing their parents, of being made orphans tonight. Aidan had to stay alive if there was any hope of keeping them together and of surviving such a tragedy. "Katie will need him most of all, God forbid . . ." Mel couldn't finish the sentence, and Nic looked similarly pained. Aidan's niece and goddaughter was special to Aidan and the perfect leverage for getting him in line.

Nic cleared his throat. "That might be the only thing that keeps him from going after Jamie."

"Use it if you have to." She held out a hand to him. "Price, thank you."

He clasped her wrist instead, the hold firm and sure. "Never a dull moment with this lot."

"Welcome to the family."

SEVEN

"J!" Danny whacked his future bro's shoulder. "Something's happening. Sonja's coming to the mic again."

Jamie's rapid-fire typing ceased, and he scrambled up from the floor. Danny scooted over, giving Jamie room to stand in the shadowed corner that afforded a view of the deck. He pointed to the right. Two of the mercs tossed the rolled green carpet from the gangway overboard as the main entry to the ship retracted.

"Ladies and gentlemen," Sonja said, regaining everyone's attention. She looked frighteningly comfortable standing behind the mic with an assault rifle. "The ship is ours. There is no way on or off."

Shouts rang out from the crowd.

"You can't do this."

"We called the cops."

"What are you doing?"

Her cool disregard for her peers and industry influencers chilled Danny to the bone. Everyone here knew her, and she still didn't care, which meant she was unpredictable, which meant his family was in grave danger. How much longer could they wait for Mel? And what could one operative, albeit highly skilled and destructive, do against Sonja and her mini-militia? He had been confident fifteen minutes ago, but that confidence was waning, fast.

"The IRA has no quarrel with you," Sonja said. "It's the Talleys we want. They can end this right now, and you can go on with your lives and get off this ship, if they'll turn themselves over."

Danny had located his parents and siblings in the crowd as soon as he'd stood. At Sonja's words, the guards and guests near each of them crowded a little closer, keeping them hidden. It was a flicker of hope lighting his despairing heart. The press did their part too, continuing to shout questions at Sonja so she wouldn't notice the crowd's movement. The Talleys had been generous with their time over the years; no press wanted to be singled out as the person who had turned on them now, even for a headline-making story. Or maybe guests and reporters alike were smartly following the FBI ASAC's orders. Cam's dark head and suited form wove through the crowd like a snake, checking in with Danny's family members.

But Sonja quickly grew frustrated with the delay and obfuscation. "You!" She pointed to one of her mercs. "Get up to the bridge and turn on the spotlights."

"Shit!" Jamie yanked his phone free of the control panel and turned on his heel for the interior stairs at the back of the bridge. "We gotta get out of here."

Danny, however, was rooted to his spot, his gaze locked on the horror unfolding onstage. While one merc left the stage, another dragged a woman up onto the dais.

Alison Mueller—Siobhan's paralegal, thirty-five, single mother of two, celebrating five years with TE this month.

Sonja grabbed Alison by her dark hair, yanking her out of the merc's hold and into hers. She pressed a knife against Alison's pale throat. "If the Talleys won't come forward on their own, then we'll force them to."

Sonja's message was clear. Talleys come forward, now, or Alison would die.

Danny didn't think twice. He started for the door, halted only when Jamie grabbed his forearm. "You can't go out there."

"I know her, J. I helped recruit her. I'm not going to let her die for us."

"You know Sonja too. Would she really kill someone?"

He glanced back at the stage. Sonja's blade dug into Alison's throat, drawing blood, as the paralegal gulped back sobs. "Until fifteen minutes ago, I wouldn't have thought so, but . . ." He threw an arm out toward the deteriorating scene.

Movement in the crowd drew his gaze—elegant heads of red and white moving forward. Siobhan headed for the stage, his father aiming to intercept her.

Sound drew his attention a different direction—boots hitting the bottom of the bridge steps. On their way up.

Time was ticking away.

An explosion, of one variety or another, was imminent.

"Danny, we've got to go!" Jamie tugged him toward the back. "She's not a killer. She's a businesswoman. Hell, the IRA isn't even in the killing business anymore. There's gotta be more to this. Let Nic find out and then . . ."

Jamie's words faded, drowned out by the blood rushing in Danny's ears. His sister and father met mid-deck, arguing. The familiar sight should have been comforting, but suspecting they were debating who would give themselves up, who might live and who might die, made the sight wholly unfamiliar and terrifying. Cam was closing in fast from where he had stood with Ellen, but he didn't move fast enough. John won the argument, and the crowd began to part as he stepped forward.

Boots thundered up the bridge stairs.

"Danny, let's go!"

Jamie's earlier words clicked. *There's gotta be more to this.* Yes, there had to be. And there was only one way to find out. Only one way to save Alison and his family.

Danny wrenched his arm free. "I can't leave them, J. You coordinate with Mel. I'm going to stall and find out what the fuck is going on. Stateroom."

Jamie lunged for him, and Danny lunged for the light switch. He flipped it on, standing tall, while Jamie cursed and hit the floor behind the control panel. Danny slapped the speaker button, switching it to two-way. "Sonja, stop this."

His father whipped his head around, as did Siobhan and the rest of the crowd, everyone looking up at him. At his feet, Jamie hiked up Danny's pant leg and strapped a gun to his calf with what Danny could only assume was a computer wire before arranging his sock and pant leg back over it.

"I'm coming out." Hands raised, Danny slid out through the swinging door, careful not to reveal Jamie. He met Sonja's henchman three steps from the top. Too damn close.

"Daniel Talley," Sonja called out over the crowd. "It's been too long."

"I agree." He broke out the Casanova smile he'd retired sixteen months ago. "How about a little chat, then? Between old friends."

EIGHT

"He did *what*?" Mel curled her fingers around the knife's hilt, nails digging into her palm. The pain centered her, kept her from blasting through the pallet of crates she was hiding behind to strangle a dark-haired, dark-eyed someone she knew all too well.

There was shuffling on the other end of the line, then after the *snick* of a door closing, Jamie spoke again, a little louder. "He gave himself up."

Through the crate's slats, Mel eyed the *Ellen* not two hundred yards away. She was on the TE dock, in the TE shipping yard, almost to the damn ship. And then Danny had to go off script, again. "He couldn't wait five fucking minutes?"

"Lynch threatened an employee. Siobhan and John were going to expose themselves. Danny beat them to it."

"And you didn't stop him?"

"Tried," Jamie said with a sigh. Not offended she had asked, just frustrated, same as her. "He flipped the lights on in the bridge. It was either be exposed too or hide and do what I can to help you. And him. He thinks there's more to this."

"Shit."

Danny was nothing if not loyal, and with employees and family members on the line, of course he would trade himself for their safety. The youngest Talley was, ironically, the most responsible when it came to TE and the most reckless when it came to his own life. Add to that the foolish notion he had developed that crashing their investigations had made him some sort of junior detective. He was every sidekick ever with more money and better clothes. And a devilish grin that had hooked her.

"It worked," Jamie said, interrupting her self-directed eye roll. "She let the hostage go."

"And took Danny instead. Hold. Moving."

She snuck from her current hiding spot to another behind a closer pallet, one that afforded a clear line of sight to the only remaining entry onto the *Ellen*. A lower-level starboard cargo hold was open, to which a mechanized conveyor belt had been connected. Up the ramp lumbered two bulging mercs in paramilitary garb and between them a third man who looked half their size and age. By the way he was dressed—raggedy jeans and a hoodie with a computer bag slung over his shoulder—and by the way he hunched his shoulders and darted jumpy looks between the mercs, Mel guessed he wasn't there of his own free will.

"In position," Mel whispered.

Jamie picked up where he'd left off. "Danny's proven useful before in these situations."

"Except he's flying solo on this one." In all those other "situations" Danny had crashed, he'd had backup—or he was the backup.

"He thinks he can negotiate with her," Jamie said. "They know each other."

Mel paused midstep, hand clenching around the knife hilt again. "Know each other?"

Jamie cleared his throat, and that was answer enough.

Don Juan Danny strikes again. Danny's flirtatious streak had helped them before. Would it be useful now? Or would it only get him in more trouble? No help for it now. She had to work with what she had. Impulsive Danny and all.

"Are they still on deck?" she asked.

"He led her below deck. He said *stateroom* to me right before he gave himself up. That must be where he's headed."

Mel inched closer, slinking from behind one crate to behind another. "Where are you?"

"Directly below the bridge. I still have eyes on the deck."

"And everyone else?"

"Cam's hiding them in the crowd."

"Can you two swap positions?" Cam had the necessary authority to make people follow his orders, but he was also a kidnap and rescue specialist. She could use that to her advantage.

"Not without being noticed," Jamie answered, affront underlying his voice.

She hadn't meant to imply Jamie wasn't a competent partner. Before he'd left the Bureau, Jamie had been a promising field agent, trained by the best—Aidan. But he had left. "You're not a fed anymore, Jamie."

"Neither are you."

No, but she was chief of security for TE. This was her job; it wasn't Jamie's any longer. "Jamie, I can't ask—"

"You didn't ask. They're my family too. Now, where do you need me?"

Point made, and no use arguing or wasting time arguing. Jamie was a valuable asset too. He'd been the Bureau's best Cyber agent, which, as she watched the scrawny young man disappear onto the ship, could come in handy.

"Meet me on the lower deck, starboard cargo hold door."

"Lynch said all the entrances were sealed."

"Except that one. Two guards just led a civilian with a computer case inside."

"Maybe Danny's right."

Between her and Aidan getting delayed in transit, Lynch's dubious IRA claim, and now the civilian, she tended to agree. "There's definitely something more going on here. I'll meet you at the door."

Ending the call, she crept to the line of crates closest to the ship and ducked behind one just as the two mercs returned to the end of the ramp, resuming their post. Twenty feet or so away. Twenty feet of wide-open, well-lit concrete with absolutely no cover. The gun in her holster and the ones at her back were tempting, but none of them were loaded with tranq darts, and she didn't yet have grounds to shoot to kill. Plus, gunfire would make a racket, and that was the last thing she wanted.

She had to approach some other way. The alternative that came to mind was pure Danny.

Don Juan Danny.

———

Twelve Months Ago

"There's no way we're getting a table in there tonight," Mel said, eyeing the packed restaurant. She'd hit the brakes a block away when she'd realized where they were headed. "It's New Year's Eve, and I know you didn't have time to make a reservation."

She had caught an earlier flight back from Boston, where, on a case-assist, she'd had to tell a family their missing daughter would never be coming home, slaughtered by a serial killer the Bureau had captured a day too late. She had shown up at Danny's yacht twelve hours ahead of schedule, just wanting to hide in her lover's arms and forget the worst part of her job. Danny, though, had insisted they go out.

His arm around her waist tightened, pulling her close and shielding her from the worst of the wind howling off the Bay. "No faith, chica."

"It's the hottest ticket in town."

"And I'm the hottest bachelor in town."

She rolled her eyes and stepped out of his arms, tapping her heel. "You're gonna pull a Don Juan Danny, aren't you?"

"Watch the master at work," he said with a wink, and despite her terrible day, she couldn't help but laugh. "Do your stealth follow thing and wait at the bar. I'll have us a table in five." He gave her a quick peck, then turned on his shiny Oxford heel for the restaurant.

She followed on the other side of the street, watching him transform with each strutting step. Shoulders rolled back, chin held higher, and a dimple in the one cheek she could see from her angle. Just before entering, he put on the finishing touches, unbuttoning his suit coat and running a hand through his thick black hair, making him appear more rakish.

Waiting for the light to change, she crossed midstreet and slipped through the beveled glass doors behind another group of diners. Danny was gone from in front of the host stand when the crowd cleared, and she turned for the bar, expecting to find him there.

A hand lightly brushed her elbow, drawing her attention the other direction.

"Ms. Cruz?" the host said, smiling politely.

"Yes, that's me."

He held out an arm toward the dining room. "Your table is right this way."

They turned the corner, and sure enough, Danny had secured the best seat in the whole fucking house. His long legs stuck out from the end of a secluded corner table for two, his arm stretched across the top of the leather booth, waiting for her. He grinned, and she bit her bottom lip to hold back her laughter, so improbable after the past few days. But that was what Danny did for her, always—brought light into her otherwise dim, sometimes downright dark, existence.

She handed her jacket off to the host and slid in next to Danny, waiting for the server pouring Bollinger into champagne glasses to finish before turning to her lover.

"I'm impressed," she conceded. "But just one thing."

The handsome devil smirked down at her. "What's that, chica?"

She grabbed his tie and pulled him nose to nose. "You're not a bachelor anymore."

———

Present

Taking a page from Danny's playbook, she ran her fingers through her short springy curls, fluffing out her hair and making sure it covered the comm in her ear, then adjusted the V-neck collar of her silk wrap blouse, exposing the edges of her emerald-green bra.

Suit coat buttoned to accentuate her cleavage and hide her weapons, she strutted out from behind the crates, shoulders relaxed and hips swaying. She pretended not to notice the mercs going for their weapons—the one at his hip, the other under his arm—and acted as if she were fascinated by the ship.

She twirled a curl and made a show of biting her bottom lip and running one of her heels up the back of her other calf. "I don't think I've ever seen a boat this big or shiny before."

"Ma'am," said one of the mercs, "we're going to have to ask you to leave."

She feigned being startled, turning a wide-eyed gaze on them. "Well, aren't you two handsome," she drawled with a smile, channeling a little of Jamie's Southern accent.

The green-eyed gaze of the one who had spoken first swept her body. Not in a heated way but rather tactically, cataloguing weak points and where she might be hiding weapons. The other one, though, zeroed right in on her cleavage.

Bingo.

She moved closer to her blue-eyed target, making sure he had a view down her blouse. "Do I look like a *ma'am* to you?"

He shook his head, but no words came out of his mouth.

"Miss," said the other, "this is a closed party."

She glanced over her shoulder, addressing him. "For Talley Enterprises, right? This is the *Ellen*?"

"Invite only," he said brusquely.

She turned back to Blue Eyes, shooting him a megawatt smile. "Oh, I'm invited."

"By who?" he asked, finally finding his voice.

She stepped closer, going up on her toes like she meant to whisper in his ear. "Daniel Talley, my husband."

His eyes flared so wide she saw white all the way around his irises, and that was when she made her move. By the time the flurry of movement was over, she wasn't looking at his face anymore. Standing behind him, she had his head locked between her arms, a hand over his mouth silencing his screams, and his body between hers and the other merc's shot. She twisted them at the last second, sending the bullet into Blue Eyes's shoulder. He groaned behind her hand, and she silenced him with an elbow to the crook of his neck, pressure on the exact spot required to knock him out. She shoved his bulky deadweight into the other merc, causing enough chaos to sweep out a leg, catch both their ankles and send them tumbling down in a tangled mass. She came down after them, a knee at the conscious merc's throat and his own silencer-fitted pistol pointed at his head.

"Who is Lynch working for?" she demanded.

"The IRA."

She pressed harder with her knee and with the muzzle of the gun against his forehead. "I don't believe you. Try again."

"The IRA," he croaked, trying to buck her off with his lower body.

"That's enough of that." She reached her gun arm back

and nailed him in the balls with the butt of the pistol. The air rushed out of him, his eyes rolling back, and he was out, going limp beneath her.

Standing, she stilled and listened intently, for the sound of any feet rushing her direction, for any chatter on the mercs' radios, for anyone gasping from the railing overhead. When she was sure the scene was clear, she knelt again by the injured merc, unfastened his belt, and used it to tie a tourniquet around his injured arm, stanching the bleeding.

She wiped the blood from her hands on the cement, leaving behind a holiday-appropriate note between the downed mercs. Sonja's men would see it, would relay the message to their boss, and if Danny was anywhere within earshot, he would know she was coming for him.

She left her rock-studded heels behind as an exclamation mark.

NINE

Danny ignored the vibrating phone in his pocket. Hip against the stateroom desk, he pretended not to pay attention as he listened to the whispered conversation across the room between Sonja and what he gathered was her number two, Paul. Sonja had the good sense to keep her voice low, but the big, bulky guy couldn't speak quietly to save his life.

Someone named Austin was being brought on board, being brought here, and Paul was not happy about it. Several conclusions Danny drew from that: not every exit was barred; Austin *wasn't* a typically Irish name; Austin *was* a typically twenty-something name; and Paul didn't want Danny in the same room with him.

Because it would blow their cover? Danny was increasingly certain that was exactly what the IRA story was. A cover. Nothing he'd overheard in the past fifteen minutes away from the deck-side crowd gave Sonja's supposed motive any credit. No mention of the cause. No more talk of blood and revenge, thank God. And no checking in with someone up the chain of command. Sonja wasn't taking orders from anyone. She, and she alone, was giving them. Not to say she couldn't be the top of the food chain, but if that were the case, someone in law enforcement or the press would have flagged her as IRA by now.

"Give me five," Sonja said, cutting her eyes at Danny. "To assess him."

A year and a half ago that sort of thinly veiled threat might have made him nervous. Not so much anymore, now that he had been tied up, turned out, and married to the most frightening woman he had ever met. He fought not to smirk.

———

Ten Months Ago

The first time Mel tied him up, she did so to make an assessment of her own.

He was feeling smug after his date with a paralegal who had taken over for one of the suspects on Aidan and Jamie's case. He had charmed, he had distracted, he had followed Jamie's install instructions to a T. The next time the paralegal logged on to her firm's server, the files Jamie needed would automatically copy and download to his probably very unsanctioned remote server.

Give him a secret society badge. He was official.

What he got instead was a pair of handcuffs hurled at his chest as soon as he walked through the cabin door of his private yacht. His hands shot up, instinctively catching the cold metal cuffs, which were nowhere near as cold as the voice that followed.

"Chair. Now," Mel ordered.

He glanced up and across the main cabin to the eating area next to the kitchen. Beneath the crystal chandelier, Mel sat with her side to the dining table, one elbow resting on the glass top. Dressed in a pencil skirt and sleeveless blouse, miles of flawless brown skin were on display, glowing enticingly under the chandelier's low, seductive light. Using her foot, encased in a stiletto that should be illegal in all fifty states, she pushed out the wrought iron chair beside hers. "Daniel!" she snapped, redirecting his gaze from where it had roamed up her bare calf. "Sit. And cuff yourself to the chair. Now."

He smirked. "Kinky. I like it."

Mel liked to exert control during sex. He had expected as much when he'd finally worked up the courage to pursue her. And he'd had no objections, the sex being out of this world. But she had never gone so far as to restrain him before.

She tapped her toe against the chair, demanding he get on with it, and his cock gave a very interested jerk. Shrugging out of his suit jacket, he tossed it on one of the leather couches, added his phone and wallet to the pile, and ditched his socks and shoes while he was at it. He'd take off his belt too if he didn't think it too presumptuous, and if he didn't enjoy it so much when Mel unfastened it for him. Striding over, he lowered himself onto the edge of the chair, snapped one of the cuffs around his wrist, wound the other through the metal slats of the chair, slipped his wrist into the open ring, and used his hip to shut it. He settled back, hands cuffed behind him, legs spread, erection nowhere to hide and pitching an impressive tent in his dress slacks.

Not one bit of shame.

He lifted his gaze—and his confidence stuttered at

meeting the cold brown eyes staring back at him. Maybe he had read this entire situation wrong. He wasn't a fool. He knew he had just done something illegal for Jamie. Was the icy tone, the hard eyes, the cuffs because Mel was *arresting* him? And not in a sexual way. If that was the case, bluffing seemed a better game plan than self-incrimination. "You wanna tell me what this is about, chica?"

"It's about trust."

"Kink is about trust."

"You're right. But this isn't about kink." She uncrossed her long legs, stood, and glided around behind him. Good thing or bad thing? Jury was still out. "It's about you going on a date tonight with another person."

Bad, then. He tried turning his head to glare up at her. "For *your* mission."

Her fingers dove into his hair and forced his face forward again. "Did you ask me before you made the date with her?"

He gritted his teeth—half pissed off, half turned way the fuck on. "I was thinking on my feet."

Leaning behind him, her warm breath blew right in his ear. "Or were you thinking with your dick?" She slid a hand down his front, over his shirt, as the other cinched the cuffs tighter. His cock strained against his zipper, pendulum swinging toward turned on. She wasn't proving the point she thought she was.

"My dick only has one thing on its mind," he said. "And. That. Is. *You.*"

"Exactly what happened on your date tonight?"

And back to angry the pendulum swung. "You don't trust me!"

She reached both arms over his shoulders and began

unbuttoning his dress shirt. "If I'm your handler, I need a debrief."

"You don't trust me," he repeated, jaw clenched, holding on to his anger despite the exquisite torture of her nails scraping across his skin.

As if sensing his struggle, she flattened her hands, palms smoothing up his torso, and dropped an achingly tender kiss just behind his ear. "I'm trying, Daniel. Give me a reason to."

Her hands went back to work, gliding down his torso, all the way to his belt, and just like that the pendulum was all the way to turned on. He was putty in her hands. He lolled his head back on her shoulder, closed his eyes, and fumbled his way through a timeline of the evening's events. "Dinner at Danko. Back to her place for a drink." Nails, painful where they shouldn't be, and he rushed to explain. "She tried to make a move, and I claimed a work emergency. Needed to check my email on her computer. Then I did the thing."

"The thing?"

"Jamie's install."

She resumed unfastening his belt and zipper. "And when it was done?"

"I told her I had to go to the office."

Mel's warm hand slid inside his pants and skated over his aching cock. "Did you kiss her goodnight?" She raked her nails up his length, the friction through his boxers causing him to groan. "Did you promise her another date?"

"Fuck no," he grunted, hips rocking up, chasing her touch.

Lips teased the crook of his neck. "Why's that?"

"Because I already have a woman."

She bit down on his tendon, and his hips flew off the seat. "Try that again."

"Because a woman already has me."

Her hand dove inside his boxers, fist closing around his cock and finally, finally giving him the stroke he craved. "That's right, Daniel. We belong to each other."

He opened his eyes. The brown ones staring down at him were no longer cold; they were liquid fire. "You trust me now?" he panted.

Sneaking a hand behind him, she tightened the cuffs once more. His cock swelled, leaking, begging for release. She smirked. "Let's get kinky."

————

Present

Paul cocked his gun and handed it to Sonja, seeming to think the extra firepower was necessary, never mind her assault rifle. He blustered out, the door banging closed behind him. Sonja approached, set Paul's gun on the ink blotter, and claimed the captain's chair, legs crossed.

Danny could have reached for the handgun on the desk, but Sonja had the rifle in her lap, and a gunfight wasn't what he was here for. He needed to stall to give Mel time to get on board, to coordinate with Jamie, and to get his people to safety. And he needed to gather information. He put on his Don Juan Danny smile again. "Not how I imagined running into each other again."

Sonja tapped a nail against the rifle barrel. "A lot's changed over the years."

"Like you in the IRA."

"Like you in a committed relationship."

He sent up a quick prayer for forgiveness, then leaned forward and said in a conspiratorial whisper, "Don't believe everything you hear."

A satisfied grin spread across her face. "I knew you couldn't lock the playboy up."

Another prayer. "You know me well." He slid off the side of the desk and came around the corner, resting back against the edge closest to her, only a few inches away. "Come on, Sonja. Tell me what this is really about."

"The Talleys are traitors."

"How? None of us were ever IRA."

"A traitor to Ireland."

Danny's gaze caught on the polished wood case, and thinking of the empty space within, his previous calm slipped a measure. "I lost a brother to Ireland."

Sonja moved the rifle off her lap, standing it upright on its stock against the desk. She laid a hand on his thigh closest to her and met his eyes, real sympathy in her gaze. "I know how much he meant to Aidan and to you. I'm sorry you lost him." And there was real sympathy in her voice too. He had told her multiple times over the course of their dalliance how much he wished he'd had a chance to know his oldest brother, how much Aidan missed him, how his one memory and the few family pictures they had of Sean weren't nearly enough.

Disgust, confusion, anger, opportunity all warred inside him. He didn't knock her hand off, the latter winning out. "Since when are you IRA, Sonja?" he asked, and she cast her gaze aside. "Were you recruited in London?"

Her hand stilled, and one side of her mouth pulled tighter than the other, a tell he recognized from some of her more spectacular boardroom negotiation bluffs. And from negotiations in the bedroom when she had teased about what she really wanted. The next words out of her mouth would be a lie.

"I am, that's all that matters."

So she was not. He was sure of that now.

He played along, hoping to trip her up, to learn the real reason she had hijacked his family's party. "All right, then," he said. "You're IRA now. What does the IRA want with us?"

"Revenge."

"With blood? I thought those days were behind them."

"Don't believe everything you hear," she parroted back at him. She dropped her hand and slid back in the chair, elbows braced on the armrests.

"What can I do to stop the bloodshed, then?" It was a question he needed the answer to, IRA or not. Hired mercenaries were on board his ship scaring unpredictable party-goers. Anything could happen. "These people are my family, my employees, my guests. I don't want them hurt." They were his responsibility.

She raised a perfectly manicured brow. "Taking over the business, are you?"

He continued to press, not letting up, not getting distracted. "Tell me what you really want, and we can all avoid more loss. There has to be something you want more than blood."

She stared him down, coming to a decision, deciding how much longer she wanted to play this bluff. She turned over her cards. "We want Steele."

For half a second, Danny blanked. He had no family relatives named Steele. Then his brain caught up. Steele, as in Remington Steele. Not a relative, but Jamie's onboard computer program, named after a fictional detective, as was his habit. The program that made it easier for TE's clients to book and track their shipments, request priority unloading, and preclear customs.

This hijacking wasn't an act of revenge nor an act of terrorism. It was an act of corporate sabotage and theft. Perpetrated by the IRA, or by Lynch Shipping? Danny guessed the latter. He also guessed Austin had something to do with it. A hacker—to copy the program or to destroy it? Well, news flash, he had a better hacker.

Before he could say anything, though, Paul burst back into the room, and Sonja's gaze shot to him. Danny twisted his torso to see the meathead giving him an evil glare, probably for sitting too close to his boss.

Sonja didn't seem to care. She stood, bringing them even closer, though her gaze was fixed on the merc and her hand had closed over the business end of her rifle, ready to yank it up at the ready, if need be. "What's going on?" she asked.

"Our two men at the entry point are down."

"Down how?"

"One was shot in the arm, the other knocked out cold."

Danny rotated back around and ducked his chin. He had a feeling he knew where this was going, and he didn't want Sonja or Paul to see him smile.

The real one. Not the Don Juan Danny one. The Mr. Cruz one.

"Any indication who?" Sonja asked.

"A woman. She left behind a pair of high heels and a note, in blood."

"What'd it say?"

"Feliz Navidad."

Danny bit his tongue, hard.

TEN

Jamie caught up with Mel just inside the cargo hold entrance, eyeing the downed mercs and greeting her with a miffed, "I see you started without me."

"Couldn't be helped," she answered with a smile as she shrugged out of her suit jacket and tossed it in a corner. "You armed?"

He shook his head. "Strapped mine to Danny's leg before Sonja took him."

"Good thinking." She handed him Nic's spare, the mags to go with it, and one of the comm devices, which he tucked in his ear. They started toward the stateroom, Mel quiet on bare feet, with only the glow of Jamie's phone screen lighting the way. They had to divert when mercs stormed their way a few minutes later, responding to their lookouts' failed check-in. Rather than engage, she and Jamie ducked into the darkened auxiliary kitchen, wanting to save the element of surprise for later, closer to their intended target.

As they waited for the mercs to pass, Mel glanced

around the industrial workspace, the ambient light from the hallway casting the gleaming metal workstations and cook-tops in shadow. It reminded her of another time she'd snuck into a darkened kitchen, only then the space had been awash with moonlight, the air scented with cinnamon, and the man at her side her brother, Gabe.

––––––

Twenty-Eight Years Ago

Mel followed her much bigger little brother into the kitchen of the family restaurant closest to their home. At three in the morning, the kitchen was long since shut down and this residential area of Miami mostly asleep, including their parents, hopefully. Out way past curfew, Mel and Gabe would be grounded for sure if their parents discovered them gone. Doubly grounded for breaking and entering into one of their restaurants.

"You know we're not supposed to be in here," she whispered.

"Oh, break a rule for once." The wink he threw over his shoulder and the hip he bumped against hers, moving her out from in front of the fridge, belied his exasperated sigh.

"Why did we have to come here?" Mel boosted herself onto the polished countertop of the long kitchen island.

"I may only be a sophomore, but I'm pretty sure prom night is not supposed to end with you coming home alone. In tears."

It wasn't, but when her date had overheard another classmate bet Mel could kick his ass, he had tried to salvage his fragile masculinity by cutting Mel down another way—

dumping her in front of everyone. At the senior prom. After she had had sex with him last week—her first time—because he loved her and couldn't wait to be with her.

Singao.

"Figured you could use the cheering up." Gabe dropped an armload of items beside her. Regular, condensed, and evaporated milks, rice, sugar, and cinnamon. All the ingredients for arroz con leche, her favorite dessert.

She grabbed him by the sleeve and yanked him into a hug. "Gracias, hermano."

Towering over her, he kissed the top of her head, then made a sputtering noise. "How much hair spray did you use tonight?"

She pushed him back to the side, laughing. "Enough to hold all the curls in place."

"So a whole bottle, then." Smiling, Gabe began preparing the food. "You want to talk about it?" he asked after he got the pot of rice cooking. "Whatever happened tonight . . ."

"No," she mumbled to her swinging feet.

"He was a douchebag anyways."

"Not that I don't appreciate this," she said, deflecting, "but we could have done this at home without the whole sneaking-out-and-breaking-in thing."

"But not without waking Mom and Dad," Gabe said. "And there's something else I wanted to talk to you about without them overhearing."

"Oh-kay," she said, drawing out the syllables. "What's up?"

He took a deep breath, his massive shoulders climbing to his ears and back down, before he set the spoon on the trivet and leaned back against the counter next to the stove. Hands behind his back, his nails scraped across metal as he clawed at the counter's edge.

"Just tell me," she said. "Don't work yourself into a lather over it."

"I want my own restaurant one day, after I finish playing football and make some money in the stock market." Her brother was a genius at numbers and on the field. A scholar athlete. And damn good in the kitchen too. Even with his hulking, defensive tackle's body, he moved around the kitchen like a natural, not like a bear caged in a tiny closet. Not like the bumbling amateur she was in a kitchen, genetics and seventeen years of patience be damned. She was far better with knives in a different context.

"Isn't it a given you'll take over when Dad retires? I can't cook for shit, and you're the golden boy."

Their father lavished praise on Gabe—and tried to arrange dates for her—at every opportunity. Advance the son, marry off the daughter. The patriarchy of it all made her sick, but she didn't want to take away from her brother's achievements, and besides, Uncle Robert was teaching her everything she needed to know to overthrow the patriarchy one day.

"I'm not sure it's a given," Gabe said. "Or that he's going to think I'm the golden boy much longer."

"Oh," she said, catching on. "This is about you being gay."

Stunned, Gabe's eyes looked like they were going to pop out of his head, and his mouth hung open like he was catching flies. She slid a manicured nail under his chin and helped him pick his chin up off the floor. "You knew?" he choked out.

"I want to be a cop, like Uncle Robert in Cuba. You don't think I haven't noticed you checking out the players' asses more than the cheerleaders'?"

"Dios mío." Elbows on the island countertop beside her, Gabe buried his face in his big hands. "Is it that obvious?" he groaned behind his fingers. "Do Mom and Dad already know?"

She put a hand on his shoulder, squeezing. "No, it's not that obvious. I like looking for hidden things. Detectivelike."

"Well, thank God for that." Straightening, he turned his attention back to the stove and added milk to the cooked rice.

Mel hopped off the island and leaned a hip where he had rested his a moment ago. "Are you going to tell them?"

"I don't know." Conflicted dark brown eyes stared back at her. "I don't want to lose my chance at this." He waved the wooden spoon in the air, gesturing at the kitchen around them. At their family's legacy. "Or my chance at playing in the NFL someday."

"And you think you're going to, just because you're gay?"

He side-eyed her as he stirred in the rest of the ingredients. "Don't be naive. I'm a half Cuban, half Black kid who plays a testosterone-hyped sport. None of the above works with being gay."

"But you are." She grabbed his arm, took the spoon out of his hand, and set it aside before switching off the burner and turning him to face her. She lifted her hands, framing his face, the fear and worry misplaced on a fourteen-year-old kid. On her brother. "Fuck 'em," she said. "Come out, or don't. Do what's right for you, and if any of them come at you, including our parents, they'll be coming at the both of us. And I'll take them down. That kid tonight at prom didn't know the half of it. I can kick *anyone's* ass."

Under her palms, Gabe's cheeks lifted, along with the corners of his mouth. "You really don't care that I'm gay? You don't think I'm . . . wrong?"

She lifted on her tiptoes to kiss his forehead. "You, Gabriel Cruz, are the most perfect person I know."

"You're just saying that because I'm your brother."

Lowering back to her heels, she pulled Gabe into as tight a hug as she could give. Anything, everything, for her brother. "Yeah, you are, and nothing's going to change that. I will always be by your side, including when you open your first restaurant."

He dodged her hair sprayed hair and kissed her temple instead. "I'll put arroz con leche on the menu just for you."

"You better."

———

Present

Gabe hadn't lived long enough to inherit the family restaurants or open his own, and whenever Mel was in a kitchen like this, her heart ached with longing—for her brother and the future he was supposed to have. The investment career, the restaurants, a long and happy marriage with Aidan, a man he proudly and openly loved, and a chance to know Danny, not just as a brother-in-law, but as the man she had grown to love and marry.

The man she could lose now if she didn't kick the asses of those coming for her new family like she had promised Gabe she would do to anyone who came at him. There was no time to waste. As soon as the path was clear again, she and Jamie hustled out of the kitchen and were back on their way, only pausing again when the light from Jamie's phone brightened.

Jamie flipped the screen over. "Update from Cam. Things on deck are tense but holding. John's calming the crowd."

Mel gritted her teeth. "He wasn't supposed to show himself."

Jamie shot her a beleaguered look. "Do any of the Talleys ever listen?"

The phone brightened again, and Jamie glanced back down. "There are cop cars and media vans converging on the dock."

Nic was up. She tapped twice in front of her ear, activating the comm, as Jamie did the same across from her. The line opened to sirens and noisy commotion. "Price, report."

Nic excused himself from a conversation and the din of noise reduced a little. "Oakland PD is on the scene."

"They're holding back?"

"For now. I told them there are federal agents on board and that we're handling tactically. But they're not going to wait forever, Cruz. Not with that many lives at stake, and especially not with the media gathering."

"Shit," she cursed, then cursed again when another voice joined the fray.

"Let me through!" her best friend demanded, rougher than usual in his Irish brogue. Aidan was struggling to keep his accent in check, strung out and on high alert after an already trying day.

"I'm sorry, sir, this is a restricted area," said an unknown voice.

Jamie grimaced, as if he knew what was coming. Aidan didn't disappoint.

"No shit! I'm Aidan fucking Talley, that's my family's ship, and I'm the Bureau SAC for San Francisco. Now let me the fuck through. Dominic!"

"He's clear," Nic shouted, then lower, for only her and Jamie's ears, "Angry leprechaun incoming."

"What the fuck is going on?" Aidan said, voice closer.

"Here, Talley," Nic replied.

There was a click and shuffling sounds before Aidan's voice came through loud and clear on the fourth comm she had left with Nic. "Mel, why the fuck didn't you wait for backup?"

"She's got backup, Irish."

Aidan let out a big exhale, his relief palpable over the line. "Whiskey, you okay?"

"Fine, baby."

Jamie didn't seem the least bit embarrassed using the endearment—never had been—but Mel nonetheless averted her eyes, leaving them to their reunion. She longed for a similar renewed connection to Danny, sooner rather than later. With each passing minute, he put himself in more danger.

Her attention snapped back when Aidan's tone reverted to short and clipped. "Good, glad you're alive now so I can kill you when I find you on that ship."

Jamie hung his head, and Mel chuckled, amused.

"You're not getting on that ship," Nic said, and she could hear the lingering amusement in his voice as well.

"The hell I'm not."

"Aidan," Mel called.

"What?" he snapped.

"Katie needs you safe. All the kids do."

All amusement fled with Aidan's strangled groan. Every bit of conflict, frustration, and dread made vocal. Across from her, Jamie closed his eyes and put a hand to the ship's bulkhead to steady himself, obviously feeling the same pain Aidan did, compounded by separation.

Nic spoke while the rest of them couldn't. "I've got an update on Lynch. She's got zero ties to the IRA."

"Sonja Lynch, as in Lynch Shipping?" Aidan gasped. "She's the one holding the ship and guests hostage?"

"She's also the one who paid off the TSA agents responsible for holding you both up," Nic said. "And Mitch."

"Mitch is in on this too?"

"It looks like he's her inside man," Mel said. "You can bet when this is over that I'm going to interrogate him as to why."

"I can't answer why for Mitch," Jamie spoke up, and she looked over to see him staring down at his phone again, face aglow in the blue light. "But I think I can for Lynch."

He flashed the screen at Mel, showing her a new text from Danny. Relief flooded her veins, then iced over as she read his message. Jamie filled in the others. "They're after Steele, the onboard software I designed. The IRA story is a front while they bring a hacker on board."

"Good luck convincing the media," Nic said. "One of the reporters said choppers are inbound, and guest accounts are already trickling out on social media."

"Any way to lock down outgoing messages?" Mel asked Jamie.

He shook his head and tapped his ear. "Not without also jamming our signals."

Another text from Danny lit up Jamie's screen.

BG incoming.

"BG?" Jamie said, brows furrowed.

"Bad guys," Mel said, and on the heel of her words, the metal deck below her feet began to rattle with incoming footsteps. She started toward another darkened cabin several feet ahead. "Aidan, Nic," she said. "Buy us time."

"You can't—" Aidan started.

Nic cut him off. "We'll do what we can."

"Whiskey—"

"I love you, Irish," Jamie said, forestalling further argument.

A pause, then Aidan reluctantly conceded. "I love you too. Mel, take care of him. Take care of all of them."

"Roger that."

Everyone disconnected, and when Jamie righted his gaze, Mel could see the wheels turning behind his bright blue eyes. "I need to get in there with Danny," he said.

"Can they hack your program?"

"Shouldn't be able to, but if I'm in there, I can also run countermeasures."

And take care of Danny. She liked this plan. She would rather be the one by Danny's side, but getting Jamie direct access to the computers while she continued to dismantle Sonja's firepower was a better tactical position.

As the approaching footsteps grew louder, Mel pulled the rest of the game plan together in her head. "Okay, we're gonna put up a good fight, but then you're going to get taken."

Jamie nodded. "And you?"

Pistol in hand, she raised her firing arm and smashed a piece of plate glass with the gun's butt. The footsteps shifted direction, heading straight for them.

"It'll look like I've been taken too. Then I'll take them."

ELEVEN

Danny swiveled in the corner chair in the stateroom, sneaking out his phone and texting Mel and Jamie when his back was to the room. It was a risk, but Mel and Jamie needed to know what was really going on. And they needed to know another innocent was involved.

Behind the desk, Austin was sweating bullets. The kid looked equal parts stymied and nauseated. A deep groove was carved between his brows, moisture dappled his forehead, and he was pale as a ghost, teeth gnawing into his lower lip as he typed furiously on a laptop. Danny wanted to feel smug—Jamie's system was unhackable—but he couldn't when Austin was terrified and obviously here against his will. What had Sonja's people blackmailed him with? A threat to his family? Or his job? Was he some IT nerd at Lynch who had watched porn on his work computer and been leveraged into corporate sabotage?

The gun in Danny's sock weighed heavily. He could use it now, while Sonja's back was turned, to shoot his way out of there. But while he could take out Sonja, could he make it past her mercs outside too? With a spooked Austin in tow? And would his shoot-out compromise Mel, Jamie, Cam, or any of the other guests on board? By staying here in the stateroom, he had the inside track on what Sonja and her team were doing. He could text another warning if the need arose.

And he could coach Austin through not losing his shit. "Breathe, kid," he whispered low.

Austin blew out a giant breath and shot him a pleading glance. "You sure you can't get into the admin controls?"

Danny shook his head. An hour ago, yes. But once Jamie had locked it down from the bridge, the only person who could crack it was—

The man being shoved through the stateroom door.

Jamie had clearly been in some sort of altercation. His light brown hair was ruffled, his bottom lip split, and an impressive bruise was blooming over his right cheekbone. He had been relieved of his tux jacket, his bow tie hung loose, and his white dress shirt was wrinkled and spotted with blood. But despite his hassled appearance, his blue eyes were sharp and alert, narrowing when Danny stood and took a step toward him. Jamie shook his head once and Danny diverted toward Austin, resting a hip against the desk's edge. As he did, Jamie ran two fingers in front of his ear, like he was scratching an itch, but Danny recognized the double tap for what it was. Jamie was wired.

"Where's Davis?" Sonja asked Paul, who had followed Jamie into the room.

"The woman with him"—Paul jutted his chin at Jamie—"took Davis out."

Sonja glanced over her shoulder, glaring at Danny. "A woman?"

Danny shrugged. "Your man did say there were high heels at the scene. I don't know why you're surprised."

"What did she look like?" Sonja asked without tearing her gaze away.

"Tall, brown skin, dark curly hair," Paul answered. "Armed to the teeth."

"Something tells me your Casanova act was just that," Sonja said to Danny, then turned back to Paul. She withdrew her phone and tapped at the screen. "This her?" she said, shoving the device under Paul's nose.

Paul nodded, and Sonja tossed her phone to Danny. He caught it and turned it over. On the screen was a picture of him and Mel, side by side, at a charity fundraiser earlier that fall. "Your girlfriend is going to blow this whole operation," Sonja said, voice trilling with irritation.

"My wife," he corrected, ignoring Jamie's slight yet sharp inhale and taking more than a little pleasure from Sonja's widening eyes. "And there's no operation if the kid you blackmailed into helping you"—he tilted his head at Austin, alerting Jamie and whoever was listening that the kid was innocent—"can't crack the system."

"We don't need him." Paul handed a wallet to Sonja. "Not when we've got the software engineer. That's the name you mentioned, isn't it?"

Sonja flipped open the wallet, then tossed it on the desk next to where Danny had tossed her phone. The wallet landed open, Jamie's ID displayed. "You want to say something for yourself, Mr. Walker?" Sonja asked.

"You threatened my family," Jamie replied. "I've got nothing to say to you."

"I wonder . . ." Sonja split a devious glance between the two of them. "Would either of you change your tune if I told you there was a bomb on board?"

TWELVE

A bolt of fear raced down Mel's spine and sent blood and adrenaline rushing through her veins. She fought the jerk of her body, decades of training keeping her still, but boiling just below the surface was the instinct to crash through the ventilation grate and end the woman who threatened her friends and family.

They had been in life-threatening situations before, but that was before she'd vowed *until death do us part*. She had never imagined those words would be so relevant so soon, and never with this many of her loved ones inside the blast radius—many of them innocents, not federal agents or headstrong lovers who willingly walked through fire on the regular.

Though even Danny was backing away from this blaze. On the other side of the grate, Jamie kept his cool, but Danny squawked enough for the three of them. "There's a *what* on board?" His normally jovial voice, the laughter in every word something she depended on after days in the dark, was full of outrage and terror, not a trace of humor underlying it. Every strangled syllable rattled her bones and made her chest ache.

"Where is it, then?" Jamie asked. "We're just supposed to believe you?"

Sonja reclaimed her phone, swiped at the screen, and held it out to Jamie again. "Locked in the engine room."

Jamie's silence was all the confirmation Mel needed. She fought another jolt. The *Ellen* was huge. The blast could have been localized if the bomb were in any other location, but in the engine room, full of machinery, oil, and other highly flammable materials, a blast could take out the entire ship. Mel doubted even the fire suppression system would be able to fully contain it.

Danny had figured those odds out as well, his usually loose frame going ramrod straight.

The merc next to Sonja rattled off specs for the explosive device, and Mel's concern ratcheted higher. Aidan's too, Gaelic curses streaming over the comm.

"That a countdown clock?" Jamie nodded at the phone. "Fifteen minutes?"

Sonja pocketed her phone. "For you to copy Steele or else the bomb blows." She pointed at Austin. "You, let's go."

The kid couldn't get out from behind the desk fast enough, nearly tripping over his own two feet. Sonja grabbed him by the arm and dragged him into the hall, the merc on their heels.

Jamie slid into the captain's chair as Danny paced on the other side of the desk. With Sonja's back to the room, Mel took her shot. Withdrawing Nic's knife, she tapped lightly on the grate and held it aloft to catch the lights' reflection.

Danny did a double take, then resumed pacing, until

she tapped again, and he froze. Jamie likewise stiffened but wisely didn't turn around.

"It's me, Jamie," she whispered into the comm.

Jamie must have mouthed her name to Danny because her husband moved so he was directly between the door and grate, blocking any view. His dark eyes searched through the slats of the grate until they locked with hers. No words were spoken, but their connection snapped into place and her throat tightened with longing. The weight of her feelings for Danny—how much she loved him, how much she missed him—always hit her hardest when she returned home from a mission.

She and Danny had thought marriage would make the hits easier, but they'd only gotten harder. Then tonight, returning late from her latest mission to a hijacking and bomb threat, she was deprived of the reunion she wanted. She needed.

One she might never get if the next fifteen minutes didn't go their way.

Sonja began to turn back, and Mel whispered, "Stall," for Jamie to hear and Danny to see.

Rotating, Danny rested back on the front edge of the desk. "How do you think you're going to get away with this?" he asked as the blond reentered the room. "Everyone out there knows you. You can't just steal our program, install it for Lynch, and go back to running the family company. You're through."

"I am. As of last week, in fact."

Danny gasped, straightening from the edge of the desk. "What?"

"I was voted out at the board meeting in favor of my clueless brother."

"How is that possible? Your profits are up."

"Not every family is as progressive as yours." Betrayal and envy colored her voice.

Mel would have felt sorry for Sonja if not for the threat she posed. She herself had come from a family like Sonja's, but she had been lucky enough to be accepted into Danny's far better one.

"So then what," Danny said, "this is revenge against your family?"

"No, this"—she tapped the computer on the desk—"is my golden parachute."

"You're going to sell it on the black market and disappear," Danny put together.

Jamie filled in the rest. "And use Lynch Shipping and the IRA as cover for your actions."

Her eyes gleamed in answer, and Mel worried at the unhinged quality of her greedy gaze.

"You're not a killer, Sonja," Danny said. "Please don't do this."

"I won't have to if you two cooperate."

Danny lifted his hands, palms out. "Fine, you win."

"Danny, no!" Jamie pushed to his feet, selling the argument. "Don't do this."

Danny shifted so he was looking back and forth between them. "It's not worth the lives, J. Transfer the files."

"You're still going to blow up the ship, though, aren't you?" Jamie said to Lynch. "It's your escape plan. Make it look like you got killed in the blast. Do you even know how to deactivate it?"

Sonja smiled, cryptic and terrifying. "Why would I need to know that?"

Whoever this woman used to be when Danny knew her, she wasn't the same woman any longer. Danny must have fully realized that too, his normally deep voice several octaves higher when he asked, "Are you going to let the guests off first?"

"Like I said, if you cooperate."

Jamie wrapped a hand around Danny's wrist and turned him fully around to face him, his back to Lynch. "Your father's legacy . . ."

"We can build another ship." Danny's eyes skated over Jamie's shoulder to lock with Mel's again. *Save them*, he mouthed.

She shook her head. Negative. She wasn't leaving him behind.

But then he laid his hand over his coat pocket, right where he always carried his lock pick set. Sonja's earlier words came back to her.

Locked in the engine room.

He wanted to go after the bomb. All her instincts screamed *Hell no!*" But then she remembered Galveston. Danny had picked a lock, getting them access to a terrorist's bomb, and Jamie had talked them through defusing it. Danny had his lock pick set on him now—she had told him to be ready to unlock some doors for her—and Jamie was right there with him. Danny had handled himself then. Could she risk his life to do the same again now?

He patted the spot again, right over his heart. *Save them*, he mouthed again, adding, *Please, chica.*

As much as she loved him, it wasn't her call to make. He had decided to risk his life to save everyone else on board. He would never forgive himself, and he would never forgive her, if they didn't do everything in their power to rescue his family and the other hostages. And she would never forgive herself either; Danny knew her well enough to know that. She had almost made that mistake before, putting her priorities over the lives of others.

———

Ten Months Ago

She couldn't shake the sight of Danny charging into a burning villa to save her. Nor could she banish the sight of Danny's disappointed yet unsurprised face when Jamie confessed the secret he and Mel had kept from him and Aidan for months—about her brother, Gabe, laundering money for the terrorist who had tried to kill them.

She found Danny, hands on his hips, in the middle of the open-air living room of the CIA's Cuban safe house they'd borrowed. He had washed up and changed into clean clothes, ridding himself of the soot and grime that had covered all of them after escaping the fire. But the shower had done nothing to wash away the dark cloud of hurt and betrayal that hung between them.

"How long have you known?" she asked to his back.

He spun, dark eyes boring into her. The couch between them did nothing to break the wave of hostility and disap-pointment—of darkness—crashing into her.

Snuffing out the light she depended on.

Knocked off-balance, she braced herself against the back of the couch.

"I overhead you," he answered, voice flat, devoid of all laughter. "Night before last on the phone, after we got access to the law firm files."

"Danny . . ."

"You were gone the next morning."

"Daniel."

"You stole my fucking plane," he roared, and she stood there, taking it. It was the truth. "The same plane we took to and from Galveston. Dammit, Mel, I fell in love with you on that goddamn plane."

She rocked back on her heels, the waves continuing to toss her around. They had only been flirting then, all those months ago. "We barely knew—"

"Bullshit." He stormed around the couch and stopped in front of her. She swore she could feel the heat radiating off him, and not the good kind. "We've known each other fifteen years."

"I didn't want to involve you. I didn't want you to get hurt."

"Then maybe you shouldn't have hidden the truth for months."

"I was trying to protect Aidan, and you, and your family."

"No!" He pointed an accusing finger at her, eyes narrowed and glittering with fury. "You were protecting *yours*. You and Gabe."

"He was my brother," she said, voice cracking. She had been keeping her promise to him.

Danny's anger waned, at least a little. Enough that he lowered his voice and raised his hand, cupping her cheek with quivering fingers. Her insides wobbled to match. "Who was already dead. How many people in Galveston might have joined him if we hadn't defused that bomb? Would my brother be doing something other than praying another man he loves doesn't die? All to protect your dead brother's secret."

She hung her head. "I was trying to minimize the collateral damage."

He dropped his hand, letting it fall to his side. "Then start putting the collateral first and not your own priorities."

He turned on his heel toward the kitchen, and she called after him, "I love you too, Daniel."

She had never said the words before, and he froze over the threshold. A spark of hope, and then his shoulders dropped, and his voice, when he spoke, was as devastated and defeated as his posture. "But you still don't trust me."

———

Present

Tonight, Danny was looking out for both of them. The responsible one; that was what her husband had become, and she couldn't be more proud. Or scared. But she had to trust him.

I love you, she mouthed back. Not a whisper for the others to hear. Three words for only her husband to see.

His dark eyes went molten before he shuttered the love blazing and turned back around. "We'll do it, Sonja."

Mel inched away from the grate. "Jamie," she whispered. "Stall while I coordinate evac."

"We'll do it," Jamie said, an answer to Mel and a repeated confirmation to Sonja. "We don't want anyone to die."

At the T-junction of the ventilation shaft, Mel lowered herself back to the ground, wincing. She had cut her feet on the broken glass in the earlier skirmish, and now each slice on the soles of her feet stung, though none as biting as the burn in her chest. The only way to extinguish it, to make sure it didn't escalate into a deadly blaze that would claim the life of her husband and loved ones, was to do her job.

Fast.

"Aidan, Nic," she said. "You heard all that?"

"Mel," Aidan said, desperation bleeding through his shattered Irish brogue. "We can't leave them behind."

"We won't, but first we have to get everyone else off this ship. That's what Danny and Jamie want us to do. Has tactical arrived?"

"They're here," Nic replied.

"Good, I'm coming to you."

She clicked off the comm and laid a hand against the bulkhead. She sent up a muttered Hail Mary in Spanish, praying she hadn't told Aidan a lie.

THIRTEEN

Taking the knife to her one remaining sleeve, Mel sliced it off, ripped the silk down the middle, and hunched over to rebandage her feet. She'd used her other sleeve to wrap them earlier but had discarded those makeshift bandages before crawling into the ventilation ducts, not wanting the fabric to snag on anything. Now on the ground again, she didn't want to leave a trail of blood or compromise her ability to move swiftly. She cinched each strip tight, picked the knife up off the floor, and righted herself.

To come face-to-face with Mitch.

Her deputy chief of security.

The traitor.

Her first instinct was to hurl the knife at his throat. But murder would only slow her down and complicate matters. She needed to neutralize the threat and move on to her primary objective. Hostage evac.

"How did you get on board?" Mitch asked. *When* would have been the better question, if he was going to pretend he wasn't one of the bad guys. He realized his mistake a second later, adding, "When did you get here?"

He had to know by now that she was the one wreaking havoc below deck. She hadn't exactly been subtle about it. But he didn't seem to think that she knew he was working with Lynch. That ignorance might buy her a minute to get into position and immobilize him, not the other way around. Several inches taller and at least a hundred pounds heavier, the older man could outmuscle her. But she could outmaneuver him.

She grasped the knife tighter as she inched around him. "Mitch, what's going on?" she asked, playing along with the charade.

"Sonja Lynch hijacked the ship," he said as he readjusted his gun in his meaty grip. "Says she's IRA and is here for revenge against the Talleys."

Mel moved so her back was to the open corridor, not the wall, giving her more room to work. "Why are you down here?"

Less aware of his surroundings, Mitch had allowed himself to be turned so his back was to a corner. "Uh, I snuck out." He fumbled for a better explanation. "I was coming down here to call you."

"Where are the Talleys now?"

"I hid them in the stateroom."

"I thought you came down here to call me."

By the flare of his eyes, he knew he'd been caught in a lie. Mel didn't give him a chance to lift his sidearm. She swung up a leg, kicking him first in the crotch with the top of her foot, then in his hunched-over shoulder with her heel, slamming him back into the corner. His gun rattled to the ground, and Mel kicked it clear.

"Twenty years of loyalty and you betray them now?" she said.

His eyes hardened, dark and angry. "Twenty years of loyalty, and when it was my turn to be chief, you skipped the fucking line."

Charging forward, Mitch tried to put his bulky mass to use. Mel ducked left, under his flailing arm, coming up on his other side and kicking him in the back.

He stumbled forward but didn't go down, righting himself and turning back to her. They circled each other, neither about to get stuck in the corner again. "So that's what this is all about?" Mel said. "You sold your soul out of professional jealousy."

"It's not jealousy. It's what's fair. It's not fair you got the job just because you're sleeping with the boss's son."

Mitch charged again, like he was in a bar brawl, and she sidestepped once more. This time, though, she grabbed his trailing wrist, bent it up behind him, and shoved him to his knees. "One, Danny's the boss now." She loomed over him, bending his arm up and back until he was cursing. "Two, I got the job because I'm better at it than you."

He wrestled in her hold. "The ship got hijacked on your watch."

"Your watch, technically."

He surged up, trying to force her back, and she rolled over his back, taking his arm with her, using her momentum and leverage to flip him. His back hit the ground, air whooshing out of him, and as soon as the shock wore off, he clutched at his dislocated shoulder, groaning in pain.

Mel stood over him, keeping him down with the point of her knife. "And it got hijacked because you're not loyal.

That's why you didn't get the job. The Talleys don't have to ask that question of me."

There was no question of her loyalty. Or her love.

The metal beneath her feet vibrated—more mercs closing in. She lowered onto a knee, knife pressed against Mitch's throat.

The show of force was unnecessary. Aidan rounded the corner, leading his tactical team. His face was pinched, stressed, but the corners of his mouth twitched, fighting a smirk. "I see you started without me."

"Your fiancé said the same thing." She hauled Mitch up roughly, handed him over to Aidan's men, and demanded a report.

"Nic's leading a team around the other side," Aidan said. "We're coming from this one. We need to move fast before word gets back to Lynch and she accelerates the clock or does something to . . ." His words trailed off, swallowed by an audible gulp.

Mel squeezed his shoulder. "We have to trust them."

He smiled weakly. "I know. They've been here before."

"We're in position," Nic radioed.

"I've got Mel," Aidan returned. "We're on our way. In position in five."

She made to follow Aidan's tactical unit that had flared out in front of them, but her best friend's hand on her arm stopped her.

"Married, huh?" he said, brow raised.

She shrugged one shoulder, smiling. "Couldn't be helped."

FOURTEEN

Danny reclined back in his corner chair, no swiveling necessary, as Jamie put on an award-winning performance behind the desk. By now, he should have cracked Steele's encryption and completed the file transfer, but he had slowed the process to a crawl. He typed slower than Danny thought possible. He cursed the fail-safe he himself had triggered from the bridge. He sent Sonja's goons on wild goose chases to disconnect this wire or that while he downloaded a decryption-something-or-other he needed, a ruse to text Mel and Aidan for an update on the hostage evac. Because while Jamie delayed the hack, the trigger clock on the bomb wasn't slowing. Five minutes, read the countdown on Sonja's phone screen. Two minutes, read the text from Mel on the computer screen.

Jamie closed the text window as Sonja reentered the room. "How much longer?" she asked.

A few keystrokes and the flash drive plugged into the computer lit up. "Copying now," Jamie said.

Danny wondered if it was Steele or something else

Jamie was transferring onto the flash drive. Sonja must have wondered too. She stepped toward them, like she was going to check, but halted when her radio buzzed with distress calls. While she met Paul at the door, Jamie lifted his chin in a come-here gesture. Danny rose and strode over to his side, eavesdropping as he went.

"Feds are converging on the upper deck," Paul said. "And they're hauling up a manual gangway to evacuate the passengers."

"Hold them off," Sonja ordered. "We've almost got what we need."

As they talked logistics, Jamie's fingers began to move faster, but lighter, so as to not draw attention as they flew across the keyboard. Danny looked down, then at the screen, and realized the words on the screen were for him.

A plan to take out Sonja and Paul, and Jamie was trusting him to kick it off. Pride swelled, as well as brotherly affection. Danny laid a hand on his shoulder in acknowledgment and to balance himself as he lifted his leg behind the desk, allowing Jamie to withdraw the pistol from the makeshift holster on Danny's calf. Setting it in his lap, under the desk, Jamie returned his attention to the computer, deleted the words on the screen, and withdrew the flash drive. "We're done here," he said, interrupting Sonja and Paul.

Danny took the drive from Jamie, circled the desk, and met Sonja in the middle of the room. She reached for the jump drive, and Danny yanked it back, out of her reach. "Don't stand in the way of my friends and family getting off this ship."

"Chopper's thirty seconds out," Paul said.

"I'm sorry, Danny," Sonja said. "But not until I get myself and my people clear."

Until that moment, Danny had kept his cool. Had pretended to be the relaxed Danny of old while shit swirled around him. Take orders and do what's needed to survive. But the rage he had banked at this entire situation—at his friends and family held hostage, at a competitor trying to steal their hard work, at the prospect of his mother's ship being blown to bits, at not being able to enjoy a fucking night with his wife—finally boiled over.

And he used it to his advantage.

"You're sorry?" He leaned toward Sonja. "My dad's life's work, the one thing my mother ever wanted, our friends and colleagues scared and threatened. People you know, Sonja! And you're *sorry*?"

Paul shifted closer, but Sonja stretched an arm back, holding him off.

Just as Danny wanted.

"Daniel—"

"No!" he barked, hand in her face. "That name belongs to someone else now."

Her eyes flashed—with hurt, with jealousy, or with surprise at seeing him so angry—Danny didn't know, nor did he care. He had Sonja right where he wanted her. He'd been trained for this situation by the best.

————

Eight Months Ago

They circled each other on the padded mats that were spread across the yacht's deck. The wave swells and blistering overhead sun added more difficulty to an already grueling daily routine. Against medical advice, Mel had chewed up and spit out Danny's ideas for a relaxing vacation with some light post-gunshot-wound rehab. He'd planned for yoga, swimming, and escalating strength conditioning, not hand-to-hand combat sessions with a fucking black belt.

"Again," she barked and slapped the mats with her palms.

God, how he'd come to hate that one word.

Hands braced on his knees, he struggled to catch his breath as sweat dripped off his forehead onto the mat. "Why?" he panted.

"Why what?" she replied, sounding barely winded.

"Why are you pushing yourself like this? You're out of the Bureau. There's no reason."

Her face fell and she quickly turned away, hiding the disappointment that was still too fresh. She grabbed two water bottles out of the cooler and tossed one to Danny. "You think the bad guys are gone?" she asked.

He caught the bottle, took a long swallow, then collapsed, ass hitting the mat and legs splaying out in front of him. He lay back, cool bottle pressed to his forehead. "The ones who tried to kill us are."

"More will come."

He whipped back up, meeting her gaze head on. "What aren't you telling me?"

She raised her palms, dark eyes beseeching. "There's nothing else. I promise."

"How can I believe you?" He'd thought he had moved past this during those hours by her hospital bed, but at the slightest hint she was keeping something from him again, the remembered betrayal roared back.

She stepped toward him, hesitated, then lowered herself to her knees. She took the water bottle from him, set it aside, and held both his hands in hers. "You have no reason to believe me, ever again. I betrayed you, betrayed what we were building, and betrayed your family." She leaned forward, head pressed to their joined hands. "I'm sorry, Daniel, more than you'll ever know. I made a promise to my brother I was trying to keep, but I should have put my loved ones who were still alive first."

He withdrew a hand and tangled it in her new, short curls. "I can't say that if it were one of my siblings, I would have done differently."

Righting herself, she kept hold of his hands, squeezing. "That still doesn't make it right. All we could have lost . . . I'm so sorry."

He nodded and closed his hands around hers. "If we're going to get back to where we were, where we were going, I need to be able to trust you again."

"You can."

"Then tell me, what do you mean by more will come?"

"It's nothing specific, nothing connected to Gabe or the case. I just meant that you and your family are high-profile. And if I take the job I'm considering, I'll be gone a lot more. I need to know you're safe when I'm gone, and that if you ever get into a hostage situation again, you can get yourself out of it."

"Which job is that?" Other than officially retiring from the Bureau, there had been no job talk for the past two months.

"Contract work, my own gig. Bounties and the like."

"And the like?" That sounded like—

"Don't ask."

Yep, better not ask, then.

She might not have talked career moves, but she'd clearly been thinking about it. And so had others in her orbit. "You've already got clients, then?"

"There's been some interest."

In a job that would take her away more and put her in the line of fire. "I have a better idea. Come work for me at TE."

She sat back on her haunches, head tilted. "As what?"

"My chief of security. The current one is retiring."

"Danny, that'll look like nepotism."

He knew she had to say it, but still . . . "Everyone in the family except Aidan works for the company."

She chuckled. "Touché."

"If you were willing to protect *your* family like that, then come protect mine and my family's legacy."

She bit her lower lip, seeming to consider, rarely making a spontaneous decision. "How about a compromise?" she said after another moment. "What if I do both?"

"I think we can make that work." He rose and held out his hand. She slipped her hand in his and he pulled her up and into his arms. "Now that that's settled, how about we go below deck and celebrate our new future?"

She looked up again, a gleam in her eye, the same devious, seductive one she'd had that morning when they'd made love in the . . . "Shower, again?"

Present

He had learned to love the word *again*, and to trust

again, and putting his faith in Mel meant he had faith in himself now. He had the skills to hold his own.

A click sounded behind him, the hammer cocking on a gun.

Go time.

Again.

With his raised hand, he crossed his body and clutched the shoulder of Sonja's firing arm. Using his other hand, he grabbed the wrist at the other end of her arm, exerted pressure in the exact spot Mel had shown him, and Sonja's hand popped open, dropping the gun.

Keeping hold of her wrist, Danny used his height and mass and the hand on Sonja's shoulder to swing her around and yank her arm up. Hand sliding around, he circled her front and yanked her back against his chest, the two of them facing Paul, Sonja as a shield.

Paul was only just lifting his gun.

"I wouldn't do that if I were you." Already standing, Jamie had his pistol leveled on Paul. "Drop the gun."

Paul's gaze bounced from Jamie to Sonja and back, gun arm half raised.

Danny clenched Sonja tighter. "Tell him to stand down."

"Drop the gun, Paul."

"Over there." Danny jutted his chin toward where he had kicked Sonja's.

"Any chance you got cuffs in here?" Jamie asked.

"Right-hand drawer." He'd put them there earlier in the evening, anticipating some post-party fun with his wife.

Gun trained on Paul, Jamie retrieved two pairs of cuffs, crossed the room, and handcuffed the merc to the railing that ran the border of the room.

Danny shuffled Sonja over, grabbing her radio before

handing her to Jamie, who cuffed her next to Paul. "Tell your men to let the passengers off," Danny demanded.

"Not unless you let us off too," she tried to bargain.

He wanted to roar "Tell them!" but Sonja was already halfway to defeated, and no matter what he had learned from Mel, Aidan, and Jamie, Danny wasn't the same kind of badass as the rest of them. He crouched in front of Sonja, hand on her face. "You don't want to kill anyone, Sonja. Tell them to stand down, *please*, so Jamie and I can try and deactivate your bomb."

She swallowed hard and nodded. He pressed the Talk button on the radio and, voice gravelly, she gave the stand-down order.

"Two minutes, thirty seconds," Jamie said.

"Thank you," Danny said to Sonja. He stood and turned to Jamie, pulling out his lock pick set. "Time to go unlock some doors."

FIFTEEN

They snatched Sonja's phone off the desk, locked Sonja and Paul in the stateroom, and sprinted to the nearest stairwell, taking the steps three at a time and running flat out once they hit the next level down. Rounding the corner, right under the stateroom, they skidded to a halt in front of the engine room.

Laptop in one hand, Jamie ran his other over the glowing red electronic lock. "The system override locked down the door."

Danny took the flash drive out of his pocket and handed it to Jamie. "Don't suppose whatever you downloaded onto this will reverse it?"

"Nope. This"—he held up the jump drive—"is what we need to deactivate the bomb. Doesn't do us much good though if we can't get to it. Who's got the hard keys?"

"Dad. He wanted to give them to mom. Symbolism and all." Danny flipped open his pick set, eyeing the bolt lock beneath the keypad. "We'll have to do this the old-fashioned way."

Old-fashioned, handed down to him by his brothers.

————

Twenty-Five Years Ago

Danny was miserable. His best friend, his older brother, was going to college. No matter how many times his parents explained that Aidan would only be a few miles away at Stanford, home for Sunday dinner each week, the center of his eight-year-old world was leaving. He sat in the middle of his brother's bed, legs pulled up, hiding his quivering chin in his knees.

"You ready to start third grade tomorrow?" Aidan asked as he fought the zipper on his bulging duffel bag.

"Ms. Mast is the devil."

"Daniel," Aidan chided over his shoulder.

"What? You're the one who said it."

Aidan lowered his voice to a conspiratorial whisper. "Because she is. But that's our little secret. Don't repeat it to anyone else."

"How are we gonna have secrets if you're gone?"

Aidan told him secrets that he didn't tell anyone else. Not their parents, not their sisters. Just him. And who would Danny tell his secrets to—like how he'd pulled his pretty classmate Sarah's ponytail—with Aidan gone?

Aidan stood and ran a hand through his bleached blond hair. The red had been showing last night before their mom re-dyed it. Another secret, though everyone in the family knew that one.

"When can I dye mine too?" Danny asked.

Diving on the bed, Aidan pulled him into a headlock

and knuckled his black hair. "Never. Dad needs at least one kid who looks like him."

"Sean looked like us."

"Yeah, he did." Aidan chuckled, though it sounded sad, like when their mother and father or sisters mentioned Sean.

He had one memory of his oldest brother, and in it, he remembered digging his fingers into thick black hair. Like Danny and their father, Sean had dark hair and dark eyes, nothing like the red hair and warm brown eyes of their mother, sisters, and Aidan.

"How about I share a secret with you that Sean shared with me?" Aidan said. "He was my best friend before you."

Danny lifted his chin out of his knees. "What kind of secret?"

Aidan scooted to the end of the bed, reached an arm out to his desk, and pulled something from the drawer. He moved to sit next to Danny on the bed and handed him a black leather pouch. It was worn, like their dad's old wallet, and the things inside the pouch clinked together like silverware.

"What is it?" Danny asked.

"Open it and see."

Danny folded back the flap and fingered the three metal items inside. Tools of some sort, but nothing like he had seen their mom or dad use around the house. They were dull and scratched; Aidan must have used them a lot. One was L-shaped and flat, one was long with a triangle on the end, and the last one looked like a key, the pirate skeleton kind. "What are they?"

"Lock pick tools," Aidan said. "Sean gave them to me when I turned ten."

Danny pulled each one out, feeling their weight and running his thumb over the rough edges. "But I'm only eight."

"You're smarter than me," Aidan said with a wink. "This was mine and Sean's secret. He taught me how to use them. So how about I teach you? You can practice each week, try new locks, and we'll race each other on Sundays. See who can do it fastest."

A new secret, handed down by his brothers. Danny clutched the tools to his chest and smiled for the first time in days. "I'll be better than you by the time I'm ten."

Aidan grinned back. "I'm sure you will, baby bro."

───────

Present

Danny had never imagined those lessons would come in handy as much as they had over the past year and a half. Thank God and his brothers for them. Kneeling, he withdrew the shiny new tension wrench and inserted it first. Using a single finger, he gently nudged it left, then right. A little more give to the left, the direction the key would turn. If he had more time, he would use the pick to test each pin, find the binding one, set it, and then the others one by one.

But Jamie's two-minute warning had Danny reaching for both the pick and rake. Holding the rake in his mouth, he inserted the pick above the tension wrench and quickly gauged the pressure of the pins inside the lock. That done, he switched his pick out for the rake. It would take a novice multiple sweeps of the rake to pinpoint the binding pin and position the others. It took Danny two. On the third pass, he exerted exactly the right pressure with wrench and rake to set the binding pin first, then each of the others.

The lock clicked.

He twisted the tension wrench left.

The door opened.

Jamie slapped his shoulder as Danny rose. "Nice work!"

Danny grinned, silently thanking both his older brothers for the handed-down secret, but his smile died when he and Jamie pushed inside the engine room and found . . . nothing. "Where is it?" he asked, expecting to find tanks wired with C-4.

Jamie was already moving, searching the left side of the room. "Look for a briefcase, probably stashed between tanks or behind pipes. Close to a fuel line or other flammable source."

Made sense. Sonja didn't need to bring fuel for the explosives when she had almost everything she needed in the engine room. All she had to bring was a trigger device and a spark. Halfway down the right side, he found it.

"Over here!" Danny shouted, and Jamie rushed to his side. He pointed at the briefcase wedged between two fuel tanks.

Jamie carefully withdrew the briefcase and opened it next to the laptop. Danny inhaled sharply. A tablet sat atop a single layer of C-4 bricks and a jumble of wires. Combined with all the flammables in the engine room, it would be enough to blow the ship. Danny thought for a second about grabbing the briefcase, finding the nearest window, and chucking it outside. But windows were few and far between on this level, and they weren't on the open sea. The briefcase bomb would explode in the Port of

Oakland, injuring God only knew how many people and causing massive amounts of property damage.

In ninety seconds, according to the running countdown clock on Sonja's phone.

"Any idea which wire to cut?" Danny asked.

"In this maze?" Jamie waved a hand at the spider web of every color wires. "No."

"New-fashioned way, then," Danny said, trying to hide his fear behind the humor. "Hack it, future bro."

Jamie fished a cord out of his pants pocket, connected the laptop to the tablet, and inserted the flash drive. The flash drive lit, the tablet brightened, and Jamie's fingers flew across the laptop keyboard. So fast Danny thought he was going to be dizzy.

It got worse when Jamie gave him the comm device with a mumbled "Need to concentrate," and Danny shoved the bud in his ear. Sirens, helicopters, and a cacophony of noise, all in mono, threw him off. "I see what you mean," he said, fighting the vertigo.

Until his world stilled with a single word spoken in his ear.

"Daniel."

He would have fallen to his knees if not for the metal strut he braced himself against. "Melissa."

"Dios, it's good to hear your voice again."

"Good to hear yours too, chica." It had been since the bridge, after Sonja first appeared. Less than an hour had passed, but it felt like a lifetime.

"Report," she said, but the order didn't have the usual snap to it. Her voice was a little softer, a little weary, and more than a little relieved.

"Jamie's working on deactivating the bomb."

On cue, Jamie cursed behind him.

Danny whipped around. "What happened?"

"Fail-safe activated. How much time is left?"

Danny glanced down at Sonja's phone. "Sixty seconds."

"I can do this," Jamie mumbled, fingers flying impossibly faster.

"Is everyone off?" Danny asked Mel.

"Aidan and John are ushering the last group off as we speak," Mel replied.

"Where are you?"

"Coming back on board to you."

"No!" Danny's stomach clenched and he rested back against the metal strut, head bowed, voice lowered. "You stay onshore and make sure the rest of my family stays there with you, especially Aidan."

"Daniel."

"Melissa, please. I almost lost them tonight. And I almost lost you. *Please* don't let it really happen." He swallowed down the lump in his throat. "Listen, if I make it out of here—"

"No if," she cut in. "How's Jamie doing?"

"Whiskey, update?" Danny asked.

"Almost there," he answered, the words slightly slurred with his tongue tucked into one corner of his mouth.

Danny leaned with his side against the strut, and Mel's gift in his pocket knocked against the metal. He wanted to believe Jamie could strike the magic keys in the remaining seconds, but if he didn't, Danny also wanted Mel to know what he had been planning, what he wanted to give her more than anything.

"Melissa, when this is over, I've got a ring in my pocket that's yours."

A small gasp, then she said, "I can't wait to see it."

The smile in her words turned up the corners of his mouth.

"Danny!" Jamie called. "I need you."

"Twenty seconds, Mel," Danny said as he hurried over. "Get them clear."

"Love you, husband."

"Love you too, wife," he replied, then did the hardest thing of his life.

He turned off the comm.

He needed to concentrate if he had any hope of ever hearing her voice again.

"What do you need me to do?" he asked Jamie.

"I couldn't crack the fail-safe," Jamie answered, and Danny's fear exploded.

"*What*?" His exclamation boomed around the cavernous room.

The countdown clock hit ten seconds and started blinking red.

"Part of the ship's security system is an EMP generator. Mel demanded it. I programmed an EMP kill switch into the mainframe."

"Why did you do that?"

"Because bombs follow us the fuck around. And as protection against high-seas hijacking. But it'll blow all the ship's electrical."

"Better than blowing up the entire ship. We can rebuild the electrical."

Jamie clasped his shoulder, squeezing. "Then hit Enter, baby bro."

Danny's heart warmed, remembering his brothers. He

would be okay if their endearment for him was the last thing he ever heard.

He struck Enter.

The comm in his ear crackled and whined, but through it he could hear Mel's anguished "Daniel!"

And then the world went dark.

SIXTEEN

Mel stood midway up the gangway, racked with indecision. Go ashore or go back on board. Danny wanted her onshore, safe with their family. She wanted to see her husband, kiss him one last time in case, God forbid, they couldn't defuse the bomb. But would she even make it to him in time?

The only other time she'd been this indecisive had been the day Danny decided on a whim they should get married.

———

Four Months Ago

She was sure they were not the first couple to have this argument at McCarran International Airport. Thankfully, though, they were in a private hangar where no one could hear the goose-like noise she had made in response to Danny's ludicrous suggestion.

"We can't just get married," she squawked.

"Sure we can," he said with a shrug. Smiling, he leaned

against the jamb of the roll-up hangar door, the sun setting over the Vegas Strip just beyond them.

The aptness of the location—where countless other elopements took place daily—was not lost on her.

On their way home from a shipping conference in Greece, they had stopped in Vegas to refuel, restock, and take a night off before returning to San Francisco. A wedding had not been anywhere on tonight's or this trip's agenda.

"Melissa." Danny waved a hand in front of her face. "Yoo-hoo." She shook her head, trying to snap out of her stunned daze. "Well, if I ever need to startle you silent, I know what works."

"We can't get married," she repeated.

"Why not?" he replied, though he didn't seem the least bit fazed by her objection. He lifted one foot, bracing it on the jamb, and withdrew a playing card from his suit pocket, flipping it through his fingers.

She paced the ten or so feet back and forth in front of Danny. "A license, for one," she said, holding up a finger.

"This is Vegas," he said, waving his card and hand at the Strip behind him. "We can get a license on the spot."

She raised a second finger. "Your parents, for two."

"They've got Aidan and Jamie's wedding to worry about."

She lifted a third. "Aidan and Jamie, for three."

"Are busy being disgustingly in love." He waved his hand again.

She darted forward, snatching the card away. "Danny, you can't just wave this off. They'll never forgive us."

He pushed off the jamb and closed the distance between

them, lifting his hands and cupping her cheeks. "Do you want to marry me, chica?"

Speechless. Twice in the span of minutes.

She couldn't find a word to save her life—too many thoughts, too many scenarios, too many emotions tearing at her heart and head. She didn't know what to say or do, indecision as good as cuffs around her limbs and a gag in her mouth.

Danny's face fell, and he dropped his hands. "Oh, I see."

Pain burned at the center of her chest, like it had that day in Cuba, like it had every day after until he'd forgiven her.

She broke through her indecision and reached out, snagging his wrist and turning him back to her. She tangled their fingers, the card clasped between their hands. "Of course I want to marry you. But do you really want to marry *me*?"

One corner of his mouth ticked up. "Don't joke."

"I'm not joking. *You* be serious for one minute."

"Oh, I'm plenty serious." He lifted his other hand and put it right over her gut, where a bullet had almost killed her four months ago. "I've wanted to ask you every day since you woke up in the hospital."

She covered his hand with hers. "Why now, Danny?"

"Why not?"

She started to object, and he kissed her quiet.

When they parted, his dark eyes shone with the setting sun and more. "Do you need another year, or ten, to know this is real? Because I don't. And I sure as hell don't need all the trappings of a big wedding to make it any more real. I just need you and your *I do*."

She couldn't help but chuckle, though it sounded

watery and choked to her ears. "Me?" She cast her gaze aside, staring at their bound hands. "I'm forty-five, I work two high-risk jobs, I'm barely home . . ."

He stepped closer, nuzzling her temple. "I know all these things."

But he didn't know it all. There was one topic they hadn't broached, and in the spirit of full disclosure—since he was, after all, proposing they spend the rest of their lives together—she gave it to him. "I don't want kids."

It had never been her job, her dominant tendencies, or her efficiency with guns and knives that scared romantic partners away. It was because she wanted different things out of life and didn't want certain other things, namely children. She liked them fine, loved all the Talley grandkids that she considered her own nieces and nephews already, but she had no desire—at twenty-five or forty-five—to have any of her own.

She should have known by now that Danny didn't scare easily. And that he was smarter than she often gave him credit for. "I didn't expect you to," he said.

She reared back, glancing up at him. "You're only thirty-three. You could find someone who wants them."

"I don't need kids to be happy. I just need you and your *I do*," he repeated, then drew up their clasped hands. He pulled the card from between them and turned it around so she could read the back.

It was a business card. For Ace of Hearts Wedding Chapel.

"What do you say, M?" he asked with a wide grin. "Will you marry me?"

Her indecision was no match for his smile and for the

shot at happiness his laughter promised. "All right, Q. Let's get hitched."

———

Present

A thread ran from her heart deep into the ship, straight to Danny's, rooting her to the spot. If she walked back down that gangway, it would stretch too tight and snap, separating her from her other half.

From the light and laughter that grounded her in a job— in a world—that was otherwise filled with so much darkness and despair.

"Boston, no!"

Nic's strangled shout broke through her careening thoughts. She whirled around, finding Cam charging up the gangway toward her. Over his shoulder, down the gangway and on the pier, a pale and wide-eyed Nic had both arms wrapped around Aidan's torso, holding him back.

Reaching her, Cam clasped her upper arm, jerking her the opposite direction of the ship. "They'll make it, Cruz. We gotta go. Now!"

The thread pulled taut.

And everything went black.

"Daniel!"

Rip.

The connection shredded as the comm in her ear wailed and crackled. Between the dark and the sound of her world crumbling, she stumbled into Cam.

"Everybody get down!" Cam yelled as he hustled them the rest of the way down and off the plank. He shoved her into Aidan and Nic, then piled on to their huddle, forcing them all down into a crouch.

Mel waited for the explosion, for the boom outside to echo the booming in her ears, the explosion in her chest.

For the final snap.

One beat.

Two beats.

Three beats.

Mel lifted her torso, forcing the huddle to break.

"What the fuck just happened?" Aidan said.

"Does anyone's comm work?" Cam asked.

Mel shook her head. After the wail and crackle, it had died. Aidan's and Nic's the same. Cam withdrew his phone from his pocket and tapped at the blank screen. "This is dead too."

Realization dawned. As she stared back at the ship, hope started to weave the strands back together. "They triggered the EMP."

"An EMP?" Aidan asked.

"I had Jamie program it into the security protocols."

Aidan began to nod, blood rushing into his pale face. "That would kill the trigger device on the bomb."

They started for the ship at the same time, only to be blocked by Nic and Cam. "Wait!" Cam said, holding up his hands. Around them, the bomb squad rushed on board. "They need to check if there's a secondary device."

It was the longest five minutes of her life. Aidan's too, judging by the way he paced and barked at everyone. Until Sonja and Paul appeared, hands bound behind their backs, and behind them, the best sight Mel had seen all day.

Perhaps in her life.

Her husband and Jamie.

The crowd on the pier cheered.

Aidan moved first, rushing past her, past Paul, and into Jamie's arms. Cam caught up to them and took hold of Sonja and Paul, clearing Mel's path to Danny. But she remained glued to the spot, afraid to believe the single brightest light of her life had been turned back on, afraid that a single wrong step would somehow plunge her back into darkness. Danny, though, was fearless. He smiled, big and wide, laughing as he strutted confidently toward her. The light shined bright, and she came unglued, launching herself into his arms. "You are a bomb magnet."

"Totally your fault."

She couldn't contain her laughter, relief bubbling out, and Danny swallowed it down, sealing their mouths in a kiss. His tongue teased her lips and she gladly opened for him, tasting traces of champagne and caviar from the party. She clinched the ends of his loosened bow tie and held him to her, savoring the much missed connection.

They only broke apart when someone cleared his throat behind them. Barefoot, she had to rise up on her toes to whisper in his ear, "Don't tell them yet."

He glanced down, dark eyes questioning.

"They've had a rough enough night." She smiled and kissed his cheek. She didn't want him to think her reticence was about him. She didn't think the Talleys would begrudge them their happiness, but she and Danny had begrudged them a wedding. That might sting a little. They should save that news for a less harrowing day. And maybe the present she'd brought back with her from Ireland would soften the blow.

"Good call," Danny said before shuffling them toward his gathering family.

John hugged her the tightest. "Melissa, you've saved this family again. I can't thank you enough."

"Danny and Jamie were the real heroes," she replied.

"I'm sorry, what was that?" Danny tapped his ear dramatically. "I don't think I heard you right."

Chuckling, she patted his chest. "You're a superhero. Is that what you wanted to hear?"

He smiled wide. "That's exactly what I wanted to hear."

The next thing they all heard, though, definitely was not.

"One big happy family, aren't you?"

Standing beside a nearby cruiser, Mitch resisted the officer who was trying to push him into the backseat. They'd done him the courtesy of cuffing his hands in front, and that courtesy wasn't returned. Mitch lifted his arms, rammed his right elbow back, and popped the officer in the nose. The officer staggered back, and Mitch swiped his sidearm. He swung it up and around, pointing it directly at Mel. "Here's what I have to say to—"

His sentence ended in a gasp, right shoulder jerking back. He dropped the gun as blood stained his white undershirt. Mel followed the trajectory of the shot.

To Nic's Beretta, pulled out of her waistband, and smoking in Danny's hand.

He lowered the gun, clicked the safety back on, and placed it in her hand. "I can do more than just pick locks."

She curled her fingers around the gun and his fingers. "I'm getting that."

He'd saved her life, multiple times over, in more ways than one.

SEVENTEEN

Hours later, Mel, wrapped in Danny's tux coat and with her feet professionally rebandaged, stood between Danny and Jamie and watched the crime scene wind down. Sonja and her mercs had been carted off in police vans, Mitch in a police-escorted ambulance. John and Aidan had given brief statements to the press before John and the rest of the family had retired to their Woodside estate. The *Ellen*, dead of all power but thankfully still in one piece, had been hoisted into the dry dock and swept with flashlights and high beams for secondary explosives. All the party guests had given their preliminary statements and been handed one of Aidan's cards with an appointment time for a full debrief scrawled on the back.

"You done?" Mel asked as Aidan rejoined them.

"We"—he gestured among the four of them, then pointed to where Nic and Cam stood a few feet away—"still need to debrief."

The prosecutor and ASAC were squared off, arguing over something, and Nic in prosecutor mode had Mel's brain rewinding even further back, to the beginning of their disastrous evening. "The customs agents at the airport?"

"Lynch paid them off," Nic said, breaking off the argument with Cam and coming over to them, the irritated ASAC in his wake. "They're in custody now."

"Debrief," Aidan repeated.

Mel barely stopped her internal groan from reaching the outside world.

Jamie, not so much. Grumbling, he slung an arm low around Aidan's waist. "It's Christmas Eve, Irish. Debrief can wait until tomorrow. Or better, the day after."

"Whiskey, we need—"

"To forget this day happened, at least for a little while."

With the adrenaline wearing off and the chilly winter breeze kicking up, Mel couldn't agree more. She leaned into Danny's side, stealing some of his warmth. "Listen to your fiancé, hermano."

Aidan's eyes narrowed. "That's one thing I'm not forgetting. Husband and wife. Since when?"

"Oh, that's my cue!" Danny said, in that over-the-top way that made Mel smile or roll her eyes. Right now, as he ushered her away from the curious stares of their friends and toward an approaching limo, she definitely smiled. "Would you look at that? Our ride's here."

Jamie's laughter and Aidan's "Tomorrow!" echoed as she and Danny slid into the car.

"Where to, Mr. Talley?" the driver asked.

"The marina," Danny said. "But take the long way."

Mel waited for Danny to raise the divider and turn up the Christmas tunes before shifting in her seat and flicking the end of his dangling bow tie. "I'm surprised this thing survived the evening."

He ran a hand up her thigh and over her hip, angling her toward him more. "You want to put it to good use?"

"That why you told the driver to take the long way?"

He waggled his eyebrows. "Maybe . . ."

Absently weaving the bow tie through her fingers, she cast her gaze aside. As much as she wanted what his wandering hand and teasing voice promised, there were things they needed to talk about, needed to say, after what they had just lived through. "Daniel—"

Finger beneath her chin, he raised her face, forcing her gaze. "You're as bad as Aidan with the need to debrief." She frowned and Danny leaned forward, kissing the frustration away. "I just want to make love to my wife."

She leaned back, cocking a brow. "Debrief after?"

He sighed dramatically, rolling his eyes. "Yes, SAC Cruz. We can debrief all you want tomorrow."

She tightened her hold on his bow tie and hauled him nose to nose. "Or the day after," she said with a wink. "And it's just Ms. Cruz now." He started in for another kiss, but Mel shot up a hand, palming his cheek, needing to say one more thing. She waited for his eyes to lift, his dark pupils and irises a molten pool of black. "I'm sorry I was late tonight. And I'm proud of you."

He smiled, the brightness blinding, and before she regained her senses, she was flat on her back, laid out on the long bench seat, their bodies pressed together. Danny swiped his thumbs over her cheeks and set about devouring her lips. She kissed him back hungrily, all the pent-up tension of the past week apart and the fear and desperation of tonight cresting, until the wave crashed into laughter. From relief, from love, from the lightness Danny brought to her life.

Danny wrestled her free of his jacket, deftly worked open the tattered remains of her silk blouse, and unhooked the front clasp of her bra. She didn't hold back the sigh of relief—having been in that damn thing for far too long—and Danny stifled his own laugh between her breasts, the joyous sound going right to her heart.

She ran her hands through his dark curls, inside the back of his shirt collar and over shoulders that had borne more tonight than she'd thought possible. She would never underestimate him again; she would show him just how much that strength turned her on. She raked her nails over his skin, turning his laughs to moans, then arched up off the seat, pressing one breast into his greedy palm while he worked the nipple of the other with his tongue and teeth, teasing it into a painfully pleasurable state. Wanting, needing to be closer still, she hitched her thigh around his waist and dug her heel into his ass, rocking their hips together and teasing them both. His straining cock bore down on her clit, right where she needed him most.

"Too many clothes," he mumbled against her skin, as if reading her mind.

"You picked a lock and helped defuse a bomb tonight. I think you can solve this dilemma."

"Smartass." Grinning, he lightly popped her ass then levered up, one knee in the seat, the other foot braced on the floor, as he shucked out of his shirt.

She caught the bow tie midair and looped it back around his neck, drawing him down so she could run her hands over his bared chest. Springy black hairs tickled her fingertips, and lean, toned muscles rippled under her palms.

He clicked his tongue against the back of his teeth while

working down the zipper of her pants. "Do I need to take the bow tie away from you?"

"Just you tr—" Her words died in a strangled moan when Danny dipped a hand inside her pants and palmed her through her silk underwear. God, she missed this; had to do something about shortening the gaps in between it. They had only been together a little over a year, married just a few months. They needed time together to grow and get to know each other better, to know *them* better. There was no question she wanted to spend the rest of her life with this man, had married him with that certainty, but there was so much good to discover and enjoy still.

Like the feel of Danny's long, nimble fingers pushing aside the silk and teasing her entrance, gathering moisture on the way up to circling her clit. He swallowed her needy whimpers in another devouring kiss, and by the time they came up for air again, he had her writhing.

"You know what I regret most about tonight?" he asked as he continued to tease.

She growled and ran her other foot up the back of his braced leg in an unmistakable message. No more teasing. "That you're not undressing fast enough?"

The pressure on her clit let up and he withdrew his hand, moving off enough to finish undressing her. His hand lingered on her bare ankle. "That I didn't get to see you in that dress and those shoes."

He shot her a devilish smirk, then sank to his knees, spread her thighs, and buried his face between her legs, tasting the most intimate part of her.

"Christ, Daniel," she hissed, unable and not in the least bit wanting to stop rocking her hips.

He kept at the delicious torture, alternating between

flicking her clit and tongue fucking her opening, until she couldn't take it anymore. She was on the edge and needed him there with her before she jumped. There had been too many solo dives lately.

She clenched her fingers in his hair and hauled him up for another kiss, humming as she tasted herself on his lips. Their tongues slipped against each other's, tangling, and when she heard that telltale unzip of Danny's pants, she used her feet to help push them and his boxers off. Danny came back down on top of her, and they both groaned when his rock-hard erection met her aching center.

Returning to her senses faster, she made her move. Bracing one foot on the seat, she flipped them off the bench and onto the floor, Danny landing on his back, her strad-dling his waist. She stretched his arms out above him and tied his wrists with the bow tie.

He wriggled beneath her. "Naughty."

Giving him a devilish grin of her own, she skirted a hand between their bodies and took his cock in her hand. "Nice," she corrected, then lowered herself onto him, wran-gling a strangled hiss from his lips as he arched his neck and thrust up into her.

It didn't take but a few lifts and thrusts to find their preferred pace, a steady rock that would get them to the edge fastest, neither of them particularly concerned with drawing this out tonight. They needed the reconnection, the tandem jump, more than anything.

She let her head fall back, hair brushing her shoulders, and Danny levered up, looping his bound arms over her head. Fingers tangling in her hair, he nipped up and down her neck. She closed her eyes and reveled in having him wrapped around her, inside her—the heat between them chasing the last vestiges of the night's fear and terror away. As their movements became frantic, she clutched his shoulders, meeting him thrust for thrust, and Danny brought their faces nose to nose. When she opened her eyes and met his glittering black ones, they were burning with the light she relied on, that connected them as sure as the thread between their hearts.

"I love you, chica."

"I love you too, Daniel."

They jumped over the edge together, laughing.

EIGHTEEN

Muted strains of salsa-infused Christmas music nudged Danny toward consciousness. He fought it, chasing a few extra minutes of sleep on Christmas morning. He rolled over in bed, expecting to curl up against his wife's warm body, and fell face-first into her pillow instead. Grumbling, he tilted his face, peeked open one eye, and gasped. Sitting up in bed, he let the sheet fall around his waist as he took in his remade bedroom. Little white lights were wound through garland and strung around the cabin, poinsettias lined both window ledges, a ball of mistletoe hung in the bathroom doorway, and laid out on the corner chaise were the emerald green gown and sparkly heels Mel was supposed to have worn last night.

And his red and green bow tie.

When had any of this stuff arrived here, and how had it all been strung up while he slept? He only knew one person who could summon all this on demand and move so quietly she wouldn't wake him in the process. Chuckling, he swung his legs off the side of the bed just as the first whiff of something cooking reached his nose. A year ago, he'd be running by now, sure Mel would burn the boat down, but through his and their friends' combined efforts, Mel was up to college-cooking competency.

Wondering what she was up to, Danny shrugged into sweats and a faded Griswold Family Christmas T-shirt and started for the door. He paused midway, spotting his rumpled tux pants on the floor. Kneeling, he scooped them up and withdrew Mel's present from the pocket.

He spun the key ring around his index finger. He hadn't been joking last night when he'd said he had a ring in his pocket for her. Only it wasn't just the wedding rings he still owed her. Those were on the key ring too, at either end, hemming in five house keys, five options for their life, their home, together. Work took them apart enough as it was; no more living apart on the days they snatched together.

————

Ten Days Ago

Danny leaned a shoulder against Mel's bedroom door. "How long this time?"

"I'll be back in time for the gala." She darted back and forth between her closet and her bed, packing with ruthless efficiency, everything in its proper organizer pouch and neatly tucked in her go bag.

A call had come in an hour ago, just as they'd wrapped another security walk-through on the *Ellen*. A lead on a war criminal bounty, Mel's favorite sort. She was off to Croatia, according to the TE paperwork he'd signed. Probably not the city indicated on the forms, but at least he had a general idea of her whereabouts. He'd had to make peace with limited information months ago, longer if he counted their time together when she was still an agent. But limited info —limited time—grated on him today more than usual.

"Not an answer," he said.

"Security clearances for the party are done," she said as she ducked into the bathroom. "Mitch will have the helm until I'm back." She returned with her toiletry kit. Danny knew it well from her nights on his yacht. "Aside from me and you and Jamie, he knows the *Ellen* best."

"Still not an answer."

She zipped her bag and straightened. "All I can tell you for certain is I'll be back by Christmas Eve." She stepped to her closet and opened the left-hand door fully. A garment bag hung from the top of her overdoor shoe organizer. "And if I cut it too close, everything I need for the gala is right here. I'll zip in, change, and be there in time for the first toast, I promise."

He pushed off the door jamb and met her at the end of the bed. "You know, this would all be much easier if we lived together like typical married folk."

"Didn't we have this conversation in Vegas? Whatever gave you the idea we're typical married folk?"

He curled an arm around her waist and drew her close. "We're newlyweds who want to spend time together, who barely get enough as it is, and of the five days you've been back since last weekend's job, we've spent twelve hours a day on the *Ellen* and wasted at least two hours a day going back and forth between your condo and the yacht. That's ten hours we could have spent in one place, together."

"Daniel—"

He kissed away her objection, long and slow, and only drew back once the tension in her frame eased. "I want a place of our own, Melissa," he said, their foreheads pressed together. "One we can decorate for the holidays and host our friends and family, a place we can run away to when we're tired of those friends and family." He drew back and flicked a gaze at the go bag he knew all too well. "You're always on the go. When you're back here, I want to fall asleep with you in our bed, in our home. "

"You said you were okay with the jobs, the travel."

The doubt in her eyes hurried his reply. "And I still am. It's not about that. I accept this is who you are, I love you for being the person who chases down war criminals as a side gig." She chuckled, and he laughed with her. He drew her hands up between them and laid them over his chest. "But you're also the center of my world, and I miss you like hell when you're gone. If we had our own place, I could feel closer to you, to us, when you're not there."

She glanced around the room with clinical, assessing eyes. "This is a place where I sleep. Every place since I left Miami has been a place where I sleep because I'm always on the go. Maybe some part of me was afraid not to be." But when she looked back at Danny, those eyes filled with hope, with the love they'd fought for. "And you get that." She squeezed his hands in hers. "I'm not afraid with you, Daniel. Find us a place to call home."

———

Present

Standing, Danny snagged a red ribbon out of the garland, tied it around the ring, and pocketed the keys. Opening the door to the main cabin area, he wasn't surprised to see Christmas had exploded out here too. More garland and lights, stockings hanging from the mantel, and in the far corner a decorated Christmas tree. And was that a present underneath?

"Did you sleep at all last night?" he asked.

She fumbled the spatula.

"Ha, I got you!" It was rare anyone, much less him, ever got the jump on her.

Mel glared over her shoulder. "You're not supposed to be up yet!"

Grinning, he sidled over to her and slid a hand around her waist, resting it on her opposite hip. "And you're not supposed to leave the bed and play Santa's helper. How did you do all this?"

She huffed and returned her attention to the skillet of peppers and eggs. "Called in a few favors. You wanted decorations."

He nuzzled her temple. "Were you going to bring me breakfast in bed?"

"No." She tried to flip one half of the skillet mixture, going for omelet, and wound up with a scramble instead. "You said you wanted to see me in the dress and heels. I was going to put them on, then call you in for a candlelit breakfast." She jutted her chin toward the dining table—set with candles, red placemats, and holiday plates. And next to his usual chair, the polished wood case holding his and Aidan's pocket watches. "You ruined the surprise now."

He reached out, laying a hand over hers on the spatula and drawing her gaze. "One, I'm plenty surprised. Two, you can't wear those heels with your feet cut up like they are." She mumbled something about worse pain before, which he didn't doubt but ignored for the sake of making his point. "And three, I like the jeans and sweater look on you just fine." He dipped his head and captured her lips, kissing her until her body relaxed against his. "Now, stop abusing the eggs, and let's eat. I want to give you your present."

"We could wait until later," she said, sounding surprisingly nervous.

Danny stifled a smile as he loaded their plates. "We have some appointments to keep today."

"Aidan's debriefs? I thought we were pushing that off until tomorrow."

"We are," he said with a wink. "Different appointments."

Her beautiful brow furrowed as he lit the candles and settled at the table beside her. "On Christmas Day?" she asked. "We have to be at your parents' place by six."

He leaned over, kissing her protest quiet. "Plenty of time. Now eat."

She dug into her eggs, but after only a few bites, she was mostly pushing food around on her plate. Why did the mention of gifts and appointments seem to make her so nervous? After everything they had been through yesterday, what could possibly rattle her like this? Maybe, thinking his gift was a ring, she was worried again about the fallout of telling his parents. But surely she didn't want to go on in secret any longer, now that the cat was out of the bag to his brother. And hell, that wasn't even all he had in his pocket. The keys and ring went hand in hand with telling his parents, like they'd talked about before her trip. But after all she had gone through decorating his place, he hated making her uneasy, would hate more making her feel like it wasn't enough. He could wait and give her the keys later, could cancel the five appointments he'd made for today. They'd find their home a different day.

"Hey," he said softly, covering her hand. "We don't have to do this now. We can wait."

She set her fork down, gaze averted. "It's not what you're giving me that's got me worried. It's what I got you I'm nervous about."

"Whatever for?" he asked, now on the confused side of the equation. "I'm sure I'll love it."

She stood, crossed the room, and retrieved the shoebox-size gift from beneath the tree. "I thought you—your family —should have this." She set it in his lap, just before her gaze skittered to the other wooden box on the table. "I wanted you to open it first in case I overstepped. I was nervous already, and then after last night . . . Bad timing."

He'd seen this woman face down bombs, mercs, and international terrorists without breaking a sweat, but whatever was in this box had beads of perspiration dampening her forehead. He picked up the package—light, just a few items inside—and carefully unwrapped it, somehow understanding he should treat it with reverence. He folded back the final flap of paper, revealing the lid of the white cardboard box, and his fingers shook. Printed on the lid was the intricate blue and gray shield of the Garda Síochána.

He had seen the symbol on some of his dad's old files— contracts they'd had with the government before fleeing. Because the IRA had attacked his family. Bad timing was right. Granted, Sonja's hijacking last night hadn't been about the IRA at all, but it had raised that specter, that awful time in his family's lives. And here was a seemingly innocuous box raising it once more.

Mel ran a hand down his arm, repeating his earlier words. "We don't have to do this now. We can wait."

He shook his head. No, if he could face down a bomb twice and live to tell both tales, he could do this. With the love of his life by his side. He snagged her hand, holding it tight and, with his other, opened the lid.

He needed both hands, however, to peel back the bubble wrap and reveal what was inside. He pulled each item out and set them on the table.

Two Transformers toys—Optimus Prime and Bumblebee—original editions, not the updated ones from the modern movies.

Baseball-like cards from the early '80s but with European soccer players on them, and stickers from the 1982 World Cup in Spain.

A white leather ball, about the size of a tennis ball, with black stitching along the seams. A sliotar, the ball used in the popular Gaelic game of hurling.

And finally, a silver pocket watch. Just like the ones his father had given him and Aidan, like the ones in the box on the other side of him. The third one that belonged in the empty spot, inscribed with his oldest brother's initials and lost in the explosion that had claimed Sean's life.

The same pocket watch Danny had played with as a child was in the palm of his hand again, decades later.

While the watch wasn't charred like the ends of the cards and stickers and the feet of the Transformers, it was covered in a thin layer of soot. All of it was.

"I tried to clean them up as best I could," Mel said, voice hardly a whisper.

Danny's gaze darted up, blurry. He blinked fast a few times, and tears streaked down his face. "How did you get these?" he asked, voice cracking. "The Garda said they were lost."

She cupped his cheek, brushing away the tears. "I hunt people for a living, Daniel. For my family, it wasn't a stretch to hunt this down."

He turned his face into her palm, swallowing down the lump in his throat. "Melissa, I don't know what to say."

"Just tell me I didn't overstep."

"Not at all. This is the best step you could ever make." He laughed, waterlogged, as he held her palm to his face and kissed it. "Thank you." He let her hand go to put Sean's pocket watch in the case, in the spot where it had always belonged, then placed the rest of his brother's personal effects back in the other box. "I think even Mom will forgive us the elopement for this."

Mel laughed then too, some of the nerves falling away. "Dios, I hope so."

"I think this will help too." He dug the key ring out of his pocket and held it out to her. "Merry Christmas, chica."

She slid the key ring off his index finger, her gaze locked on the canary yellow diamond on one end. "Danny, it's gorgeous."

"I caught you eyeing it last time we were getting Aidan's and Jamie's rings sized."

"I paused for maybe five seconds."

He shrugged, leaning back in his chair and crossing one leg over the other. "I noticed."

She admired his ring next. A platinum band with a matching yellow diamond cabochon in the center. "Yours is gorgeous too."

Finally, she got to the keys, flipping through them. "And these?"

"Those are our appointments today."

"Appointments for what?" She lifted her gaze, eyes wide.

"Our future home."

Her eyes widened impossibly farther, round as saucers. "Five of them?"

Laughing, he leaned forward and pecked her pursed lips. "We'll pick one. But I bribed the realtor to give me five options to tour today. No more living apart, Mel. We find our home, we tell the family tonight, and we grab hold of every day, every minute we can get together."

She looked down at the keys in her hand, and his heartbeat skipped, worrying now if he had overstepped. But a moment later, she closed her fingers around the keys, clutching them tight, and threw her other arm around his neck, drawing him in for a deep kiss. "We are definitely blowing off all debriefs today."

"I like the way you think, wife."

"Not as much as I like you, husband."

Grinning against her lips, he slid off his chair onto his knees and drew her onto the floor with him.

They were late for their first appointment.

NINETEEN

Mel strolled around the edge of the Talley great room, taking in her family as Gaelic Christmas tunes filled the big manor house. Redheaded children were scattered across the floor tearing through presents. John, Aidan, and Siobhan stood on the opposite side of the room, placing bets on bowl games. Cam flirted with Grace in the kitchen, with Jamie in there too, giving his best friend a hard time and putting the finishing touches on dinner. Danny sat sandwiched between his mother and his other sister, Chloe, on the couch, flipping through house pictures on the iPad, getting their votes on the top contenders.

And the box of Sean's personal effects rested on the mantel, atop the case of pocket watches, in a place of honor.

Danny had been right. Bringing those pieces of Sean back to them had softened Ellen up enough that she forgave their elopement. For now. Mel suspected some part of Ellen would always hold "running off with her baby to get married" against her. Maybe she would offer to officiate at

Jamie and Aidan's wedding to chip away a little more at that grudge.

She was still turning the thought over as she wandered out of the great room to the house's inner courtyard. At the long wooden table beneath the vine-covered trellis sat the last of their friends, alone and nursing a beer.

Mel slid into the chair next to him. "Price."

He acknowledged her with the tip of his bottle. "So the secret's out?" he asked, eyeing the yellow diamond on her finger. "Congrats, officially."

She spun the ring around her finger, smiling, until she noticed the troubled look on his face. "So why aren't you inside celebrating with us?"

He took another pull on the beer. "I don't really know what to do with . . . around . . ." He waved his other hand in the air. ". . . Family."

"You're not spending Christmas with yours," she said, an observation, not a question.

"I don't want anything to do with mine if I can help it."

She nudged his shoulder. "Well, you're in luck. This one likes strays, if that's not already obvious."

"Hey!" Gravel crunched underfoot, and both their gazes whipped up. Cam stood in the kitchen doorway, shoulder against the jamb, beer bottle dangling from his fingertips. "Who you calling a stray?"

Mel chuckled. "I was referring to the three of us."

Jamie appeared behind Cam. "Make that four."

"Please," Cam guffawed. "At least you have the money to fit in with this lot."

"And you have the Irish name and propensity to get shot at." Jamie clapped his shoulder. "You fit right in."

"Ain't that the truth," Aidan said as he and Danny joined them outside.

She was about to call him out on picking up his fiancé's Southernisms when she noticed the shot glasses in Aidan's hands and the wrapped gift in her husband's. "What've you got there?"

"A wedding gift," Cam said. "From all of us."

Jamie smiled. "You didn't think you were going to get away without a toast, did you?"

"I'm more worried about this than I was about Mom," Danny said, lowering himself into the chair beside her. "Ai says you should open it."

"Meaning it's really for you," Aidan said with a wink.

Dubious and curious, she sliced through the tape with her nails and found a wonderful surprise inside what appeared to be a whiskey box.

Tres, Cuatro y Cinco, an excellent, rare blend of tequila.

"I haven't had this in years." She ran her hand over the long, tall bottle, thumb tracing the hand-signed label, before glancing up and smiling at each of her friends. "Thank you."

"Crack it open," Danny said. "Let's give this one a taste."

She twisted the cap, tore the seal, and yanked out the stopper. She filled each glass and Danny passed them out, all of their friends now on their feet.

Cam raised his glass first. "May no more bombs be in your future."

"Hear, hear!" they all said before taking a sip.

Then Nic. "May you always fight for, and never against, each other."

"Hear, hear!" Another sip.

Mel reached out, twining her fingers with Danny's.

From Jamie. "May you always find your way home to each other."

"Hear, hear!" Another.

Danny's eyes locked with hers.

And last from Aidan. "May you always remember you are loved, by each other and your family. And may you never again keep another secret like this from your family if you value your lives."

"Hear, hear!" This time their voices were accompanied by a chorus. Around them, the entire rest of the family had drifted out, looking on as they toasted.

Everyone laughed, but then quieted when Danny lifted his glass. "To my wife and partner, the woman I'd trust with my life."

"Hear, hear!" echoed around them once more, but Mel only had eyes for her husband. "And to you, my husband, the man who makes my soul laugh. I trust you, with everything."

Danny smiled, so big and warm, so full of the light she needed to find her way out of the darkness, to find her way home. Arm around her waist, he drew her into a back-bending kiss, the laughter on his lips filling her soul. And all around them, their family cheered, "Hear, hear!" and "Feliz Navidad!"

———

Reviews are an invaluable tool when it comes to spreading the word about great reads. Please

consider leaving an honest review for *Tequila Sunrise*
on your favorite review site.

Thank you for reading!

ACKNOWLEDGMENTS

First Edition Acknowledgments:

First and foremost, thank you readers for making my debut year as a published author amazing! You've welcomed me and Agents Irish and Whiskey into your lives and hearts, and I hope with this holiday novella, you'll make some room for Mel and Danny too. I've wanted to tell their story since first flirt and had an absolute blast weaving love, action and humor together for them.

Many thanks to Deb Nemeth, Angela James, the Carina/HQN Teams and Laura Bradford for helping me expand the AIW 'verse and for continuing to provide amazing support in all aspects of this publishing journey. It's a true pleasure working with you all.

Thanks also to Kristi Yanta for the A+ plotting and pacing advice, to Keyanna Butler for being an awesome sauce PA, and to Judith at A Novel TakePR for taking my PR vision and running with it.

And finally, all the eggnog (spiked, of course!) and holiday cookies (that I didn't bake!) to my writing groups and writing sprint partners. You keep me afloat with your boundless encouragement and ready access to caffeine. Thank you!

Second Edition Acknowledgments:

Among my readers, it is a well known fact that Mel runs the Whiskey Verse. She is my favorite heroine and tied with Nic as my favorite character I've written. So when it came time to do the second edition of her and Danny's story, I wanted Mel front and center on the cover—and the model had to be perfect. I have looked for *years* for my Mel. I was afraid when the time came, I wouldn't find her. Enter photographer Lindee Robinson and model Ashley with the save. So perfect! And Cate worked her magic as usual with the cover.

Thanks as well to the others who helped pulled this second edition together: Adam and Sandy on editing, Kim and Rachel on beta, and Nina and the VPR Team on PR. And thank you, readers, for continuing to love Mel and Danny as much as I do! These two characters bring me such joy to write, whenever they pop up. I'm glad they bring you the same.

ALSO BY LAYLA REYNE

For the most up-to-date list of titles and a helpful reading order, please visit www.laylareyne.com.

Dead Draw

Bad Bishop

King Hunt

Soul to Find:

Icarus and the Devil

Changing Lanes:

Relay

Medley

Freestyle

Table for Two:

The Last Drop

Blue Plate Special

Over a Barrel

Standalone Titles:

Dine With Me

Variable Onset

Sweater Weather

What We May Be

ABOUT THE AUTHOR

Layla Reyne is the author of *What We May Be* and the *Agents Irish and Whiskey*, *Fog City*, and *Perfect Play* series. A Carolina Tar Heel who spent fifteen years in California, Layla enjoys weaving her bicoastal experiences into her stories, along with adrenaline-fueled suspense and heart pounding romance.

You can find Layla at laylareyne.com, in her reader group on Facebook—Layla's Lushes, and at the following sites:

BB bookbub.com/authors/layla-reyne

f facebook.com/laylareyne

⊙ instagram.com/laylareyne

♪ tiktok.com/@laylareyne

Made in the USA
Columbia, SC
10 September 2023

22668153R00093